Write Michigan
2023-2024 Anthology

Chapbook Press

Schuler Books
2660 28th Street SE
Grand Rapids, MI 49512
(616) 942-7330
www.schulerbooks.com

Write Michigan 2023-2024 Anthology

ISBN 13: 9781957169774

Gary D. Schmidt
Joshua Boers
Kelly Selby
Samantha Engel
Nathan Grajek
Heather Picardat
Maggie Roberts VanHaften
Sonja de Wilde
Finn Rice
Eli Ferguson
Jordan Fletcher

Katelyn Messina
Lucy Yoder
Leyla Köroğlu
Nora Sportel
Elena Hood
Rylan Day
Emma Krueger
Hunter Miller
Rylan Day

Printed in the United States by Chapbook Press.

Table of Contents

Foreword

By Gary D. Schmidt

In my junior year of high school, our French class—which had been together since first grade—began to study the works of the great nineteenth-century European authors. Our language skills, after nine or ten years of study, were not terrible, and Madamoiselle Kumpikas was confident enough to explain that cribs—that is, English translations—were never, ever to be used, on pain of something horrible. We believed her; she was that kind of teacher. And so we began to read the short stories of Guy de Maupassant en français.

We began with "Le Parure," a short story in which a vain and somewhat ambitious woman borrows a diamond necklace from a high society friend so that when she attends a formal dinner party, she will look as elegant and wealthy as she someday hopes to be. But disaster: Madame Loisel somehow loses the necklace. She and her husband replace it with a new one, but the cost is tremendous, and the loans that they take out, and the sale of most of their possessions, and their desperate grasping after the most menial jobs, leave them devastated financially; they are plunged into terrible poverty.

Ten awful years go by, and by chance Madame Loisel—now not even recognizable as the woman she had once been—meets the woman from whom she had borrowed the necklace, and since the debt is finally paid off, she tells her the story of the necklace.

Translating this for the first time, I had no idea how the story would end. How could this possibly come out right? So when Madame Loisel learned that she had actually borrowed "une fausse rivière de diamants," and the story ended without anything else, I couldn't understand what Maupassant was saying. What I had translated had to be wrong—a faux river or stream of diamonds? What was a false river? Obviously—and especially since the story ended on this sentence—it couldn't be that the diamonds were faux. So what did a river have to do with it? And why did the story end with that? Was it some unaccountable metaphor?

I went on to the second story: "Boule de Suif." I translated it as "Ball of Fat," though it seemed an unusual title. Again, the ending confused me.

Could these characters, who were all so sympathetic, really have changed so abruptly at the end? Impossible. No one would write a story where something like this would have happened. That whole betrayal scene, which ends with Boule de Suif weeping in the corner, couldn't be what it seemed to be, right? So where had I gone wrong?

I figured my translations were not particularly good and did the unthinkable: I walked down to Cherry Hill Books, bought an English translation of Maupassant's short stories, and read them. I learned two things. First, sometimes you should just trust your translations. Second, short stories—I mean, great short stories—can challenge everything you know about your world. They can make you gasp with surprise. They can show you a humanity capable of things—good and ill—that you had never imagined they might be capable of doing. They can—in the words of a good friend and colleague—give you more to be a human being with.

That day, with my illegal translation of Maupassant, I learned that.

I stayed up most of that night reading the rest of his stories and haven't put them down much since. I still use my Cassell's New Compact French Dictionary, taped together and generously rubber-banded, when I need to. But that night, I read them like someone who was understanding something big about the world for the first time.

The short story as a form is relatively new, in comparison to the other forms that literature has enjoyed. Poetry in the West is as old as David's Psalms, drama as old as ancient Greece. Prose rhetoric enjoyed one of its golden ages in Rome. The novel is sort of an early adolescent. Though some argue that it found its beginnings in the eighteenth century, others have argued that it appeared in English earlier with Sir Philip Sidney's *Arcadia*—a Renaissance work.

The short story, on the other hand, is like a kid in middle school; in the United States it came into its own in the nineteenth century. Suddenly there were stories like "Rip Van Winkle" and "The Legend of Sleepy Hollow" by Washington Irving, "My Kinsman, Major Molineux" by Nathaniel Hawthorne, "The Tell-Tale Heart" and "The Pit and the Pendulum" by Edgar Allen Poe, and then this amazing whitewater rush into the twentieth century with Kate Chopin and Charlotte Perkins Gilman and Jack London and Edith Wharton and Willa Cather and Ernest Hemingway and Zora Neale Hurston and Langston Hughes and Flannery O'Connor and a whole host of writers who perfected the form of the short story and turned it into the literary phenom that it is today: a gem of a form so perfect in its size and impact that it, like a sonnet, astonishes a reader in doing what it does within the strict confines that govern it.

And what are those confines? Above all, space. In terms of fiction, space as confined and narrow as a haiku.

Back to Maupassant.

In "Le Parure," the characters are working within a very small space indeed. Madame Loisel wants to impress those she will meet at a formal dinner party, so she borrows what she believes to be an expensive necklace to look the part. She loses the necklace, spends a decade in poverty to pay it back, and discovers that the necklace was only paste. The problem is clear and simple, the plot line direct and unambiguous, the conclusion established abruptly since the reader can infer all that follows, the pleasure derived from the unexpected twist at the end. Thus a short story.

But in "Ball of Fat," the space of the story is very different. There are a number of characters on the coach—each has to be established so as to be not just a crowd, but a collection of individuals, each with their own clear identity. They are refugees, fleeing an invasion, and are stopped by an official from proceeding beyond a checkpoint. Maupassant has to establish the historical and cultural moment and then suggest a connection between the external conflict and the internal conflicts that mark the characters. The story is sharply focused on the changes in attitudes that the so-called proper members of society in the coach undergo as they are inconvenienced by the official's interest in, and refusal to move on from, the member of their party with the least social standing.

This is a story with a much larger historical context, with more characters, with changing positions among those characters, with a single prominent character who is always acted upon, and, in the end, with a powerful question: How do we treat the weak and powerless within our communities?

What is astonishing here is that both of these stories—one so simple in structure and plot line, the other so very complex—take place in about the same number of pages: that is, less than most chapters in a novel.

In a short story, the confines of space do not reduce complexity of plot or meaning, simplify characters, or limit the kinds of issues the story can accommodate. As with a fourteen-line sonnet, that limited space is what creates the boundaries that amplify the story's meaning.

But the confined space does more than amplify.

"Le Parure" ends with Madame Loisel being told that the necklace she had lost was worth only five francs—hardly anything at all. It's the very last line of the story. Madame Loisel and her husband had worked ten years in poverty to pay back something that was worthless. Aside from the larger thematic meaning that is suggested here—how much time do we waste working for what is ultimately worthless—the abrupt ending leaves huge questions. We are not given, for example, Madame Loisel's reaction to this news. Is there rueful laughter? Is there weeping despair? Is there anger, however undeserved, toward the woman who lent her the necklace? Does she faint away?

Does she run home and tell her husband the news? How would he receive it?

And how about this: Does the woman who lent her the necklace still have it, having thought that it was worth only five francs? Does she give it back to Madame Loisel now, recognizing that it's an immensely valuable necklace? If so, do they sell it? What do they do with the money? Has Madame Loisel learned anything? Has she changed? Will this shift in her fortunes come with new wisdom about how it is that we live in this world?

Has Madame Loisel grown?

The confining quality of the short story form means that we as readers will never have Maupassant's responses to these questions, because he has left the answers to the reader. And as the reader ponders those questions and considers their potential answers in the context of what is known about the characters, the reader begins to construct answers. Or to put it another way, the form of the short story invites readers to help create not only the plot but also the meaning of the story. If, for example, the reader believes that Madame Loisel will descend into mere bitterness, that suggests one meaning for the story; if however she moves toward self-knowledge and perhaps generosity to those around her, that is another meaning; if she moves toward a rejection of social ambition and its emptiness, that suggests a meaning that centers on greater wisdom . . . and so on.

And as readers contribute to the meaning of the story, the form suggests powerfully that all fiction follows the timeline of a broken life or a broken set of lives. Fiction does not deal with total happiness.

Fiction deals with human response to a world in which hurt is common, misunderstandings are the norm, and anger and fear live in the evening news. This is not cynicism; it is the heady and wonderful belief that long and short fiction can, in unique ways, speak to our human situation, with the understanding that the human situation is implacably placed in time. If we place a bracket at the beginning of a novel—say, by a kiddo who is eight years old—and then another bracket later on—say, a character of forty or so who realizes that he has gone the wrong way—then we are looking at a story that spans more than thirty years, in which a character may, for example, move little by little from innocence to experience. The novel form gives the writer that luxury of time to follow change and evolution.

But the short story form is not so generous. Its brevity reflects the brevity of the passing time of the work where the reader is granted only this short while, these few pages, to be struck by an acute moment—not thirty years, but a moment—when everything changes for a character, everything becomes sharper, everything is now suddenly clear, or everything falls apart—and the reader is left to consider what follows—and what that means for us mortals. In a short story, the brackets are close together—and the writer is working within them, shoulder to shoulder.

And perhaps in the end, that is why we marvel at the gem of the short story form. A lifetime fits into it, though it's held in a moment. And to pull that off while focusing on plot and characterization and setting and tone and language and point of view—that's a fantastic leap of art.

So, you sit down to write and wonder how close you can bring the brackets. You only have three thousand words—just a little longer than this foreword. And now, here's my character and here's the situation: she's thinking about her aging mother, sitting out in the yard, kept warm in the sun with an afghan over her lap. So what happens next? Well, my character is walking out the screen door, past the lilacs that her mother and father had planted in front of the clapboard house soon after she was born, only a few days before the husband died too young, the husband who had held his wife's soiled hand when they had finished the planting, and they had stood for a moment to admire the new stalky plants, and funny thing, they couldn't remember if the lilacs were going to be purple or pink or white when they bloomed—but that was okay. That was okay. They had all the time in the world to find out.

About the Author

Gary D. Schmidt is an award-winning children's book author. He received a Newbery Honor and a Printz Honor for his young adult novel *Lizzie Bright and the Buckminster Boy* as well as a Newbery Honor for *The Wednesday Wars.*

Adult Judges' Choice Winner

Gambler's Rest
Joshua Boers

Anyone else walking through the fabled batwing doors of Gambler's Rest would have taken one look at the ghoulish inhabitants and turned around, resolving to seek friendlier company among the wolves and rattlesnakes of the forest.

But Lonnie had come too far for that.

A soldier in moldering bronze armor, double-headed ax protruding from his face, set down his dice and fixed Lonnie with a stony, one-eyed gaze. The man he was throwing against, an ashen-faced starveling covered by the barest threads of a loincloth, mirrored the gesture— neck purple with the evidence of strangulation. A motley assortment of outlaws, knights, and sailors—all dead, all *horrible*—put their cards aside to leer at the intruder.

Lonnie didn't care. He barely saw them.

He had traded stories with sharps and swindlers across the territories, consulted maps, searched forests acre by acre, and dug up no less than three graves—each one an unadorned wooden cross marking the ignominious resting place of a man killed with cards in hand. He had found the way, alive. And though a hundred faces stared at him, he was interested in only one.

Lonnie stepped forward and the doors swung shut behind him, doing nothing to keep out the biting winter wind—indeed, it was colder inside than out. His eyes flitted from table to table, eliminating each as a possibility. He lingered on a face, hoping it was hers—but it was some other dead woman, with a curse in her eyes, and for a moment he could not look away. Terror and despair gripped him and he cast his eyes upward, away from the horror on all sides—and there she was.

A woman, standing stock-still, with braided brown hair and an oval face.

Bloodless bullet wounds in her chest and shoulder. She stood on a balcony that coiled endlessly into the sky, shoulder-to-shoulder with other dreadful specimens—headless, limbless, drowned, burned—and though dirt-brown icicles hung from the ancient banisters, Lonnie could not see her breath.

"Evelyn!" he shouted. "Lonnie!"

It was the way she always used to say it. Every husband's name gets sanded down to a pattern by years of familiar use. The "ah," flat and extended, dropped into the "ee" at just the right moment, and Lonnie realized that no one had said his name quite right for ten years.

But Evelyn had not moved her mouth.

It was not her voice.

Behind him.

Lonnie turned and had no trouble picking out the one who spoke. Every gambler still watched him, but one man had fire behind his eyes. He wore a faded blue soldier's uniform—not the Union bluecoat, but something older that Lonnie could not identify. Ragged golden epaulets clung to his shoulders and tarnished silver buttons lined his front. He sat at a poker table with dead men, but seemed almost alive. More than alive. The others moved slowly, stared without intelligence, gripped cards with stiff fingers.

This man—though a deep triangular wound to the neck proved he was one of the dead—positively glowed.

"Evelyn isn't there anymore," he said. "What happened to her?" said Lonnie.

The man raised his hand—a sweeping gesture that dismissed his companions from the table. He was too animated for this place. It was his eyes more than anything—swirling, burning,

shifting and blinking constantly—somehow expressing too much. His entire existence seemed in poor taste. He pointed toward an empty chair, then began gathering cards back into the deck.

"Do you know what we play for here?" said the man. "What happened to Evelyn?" said Lonnie.

"I'm getting there! Look at the table. What's missing?"

The old table was worn and stained. The surface of the wood was cracked, and through the cracks Lonnie could see history—gilt-bronze, alabaster stone—surfaces through time. It was less of a table than it was the idea of a table. It was empty except for a pair of bronze scales. No food, no drink, no money.

Nothing to bet with.

"You can't imagine how boring it is to be dead," said the man, hitting the table. "A gambler killed with cards in hand can't find his way to heaven. We end up in this place—neither here nor there. Unresolved, like a coin in the air. Some unlucky souls have been here for thousands of years. We're stuck here with our lives behind us, and there's only one currency— memory.

The man tapped his head.

"New memories don't stick well in a dead brain. All we can do, forever, is gamble for other people's memories. And I'm the best gambler here.

That's why Evelyn stands on the balcony with the unmoving dead—I won her memories. She overplayed her hand. Now she's in my head."

Lonnie had heard of this place—he had gathered scraps of legends, tall tales, half- forgotten songs and stories—but he had heard nothing about this. He met the dead man's ever- blinking eyes, but they were unreadable, even to him.

"I don't believe you."

"I knew your name, didn't I? I remember traveling with you from town to town. I know all your little signals for fixing card games—and I know you're hopeless at poker without them. I know every one of your tells. And I know that despite all this, once I tell you that you can win Evelyn back, you'll risk everything to do it. Even though you'll lose."

Lonnie sat, watching the man closely. The man pulled a silver coin out of the interior pocket of his coat. On one side there was a lion holding a sword, on the other there was a crown and a foreign script Lonnie could not read.

"Tell me how to win her back."

The man moved the set of scales so it was directly between them.

"I'll show you. Think of a memory."

"What?"

"Something small to start. You walked through the snow on your way here. Think of the cold. I haven't been cold for years."

Lonnie remembered his walk to the door—the sting in his ears, the crunch of the snow underfoot, the wind howling through the trees and gnawing his skin—and as he concentrated, his side of the brass scale began to descend, as if weighed down.

The man nodded.

"I remember running through a desert valley once, sword at my side, with an army of swift men. There was somewhere we had to go. I don't know what came before or after—this is an old memory, not one of mine—but the stone was sharp and I remember the cry of the birds. I'm through with it."

The brass scales equalized.

"50/50 odds," said the man. "No tricks, just luck. Men have gambled this way since before the beginning of history. Some of the dead here still roll sticks and bones, though they barely remember why. But I remember."

The man held the coin in front of him.

"Call it. Lion or line? Heads or tails?"

"Tails."

The man flipped the coin, and as it hung in the air, Lonnie could feel the outlines of both memories superimpose—the urgency of his walk to the saloon door, the desperation of the desert run, the bitter cold, the beating sun, the aching legs, the hunger, the fear. Then the man caught the coin, slapping it on his wrist with more dexterity than was appropriate for a dead man.

Heads.

And suddenly Lonnie's mind was empty. He looked frantically around the room—face to horrible face, table to moldering table, balcony to forbidding balcony—grasping for details like a drowning man grasping for driftwood. He was in Gambler's Rest. He had crossed to the world between worlds, he had passed through the saloon door—but everything between those memories was gone.

The man staggered back as if he had been shot, then shivered with cold—or maybe pleasure.

"That's the stuff!" he said. "That packs a wallop! I've played for dead memories, but a living memory? I felt that in my bones!"

He snatched up the deck of cards and began to shuffle them, speaking quickly.

"You could give Evelyn all her memories back and walk out of here together—you just have to win them from me first. Five-card draw is your game, right? Don't bother answering. I know everything about you."

Lonnie was himself again, but there was an absence inside him and it was sending him into a panic. He took a long, shuddering breath—willing his heart to stop racing, fighting to remain rational.

"How do I know you have all of Ev's memories?"

"I'll tell you. It's because I know the way out. I have no use for it—I've won lifetimes of memory, reduced these people to almost nothing. I'm more alive here than I'd ever be on earth. You must have found the way, too—after all, you came here alive. But Evelyn didn't know the way. So she gambled every treasured moment, every single one of her memories, trying to get back to you. You should feel flattered."

"Where did we meet?"

"A steamboat. In Montana."

"Where did we get married?"

"Lago."

"What was the last thing she said to me?"

"I don't remember. 'Pass the water,' I think. It didn't seem important at the time. Isn't that the way? They never know what's about to happen.

There's never any time to prepare." Lonnie was breathing very hard now.

He tried to read the man's face again, but it was inscrutable. Hundreds of scraps of personality danced behind his eyes, informed by thousands of years of memory. With every blink, they shifted—expressing something new. Something more than human.

The man shoved the cards toward Lonnie.

"Cut the deck," he said.

Ten years ago Lonnie might have been able to cheat—misdirect the man and fix the deck somehow. His hands had been quick—quicker than most men's eyes, if they weren't watching too closely. But his fingers had lost their memory. He had hardly touched a deck of cards in all that time—not without Evelyn. He needed a partner. She had the head for numbers and the heart for danger. After what happened, how could he carry on alone?

The man watched closely as Lonnie cut the deck, as though he could tell what Lonnie had been thinking—or knew him so well that he could guess.

"Ante up," said the man.

But Lonnie could not think of a single memory trivial enough to risk. He remembered so much—great triumphs and awful tragedies, each one essential to the story of their lives. He tried to focus on one normal day, starting from the beginning. Something mundane.

"Coffee. Coffee together."

Even before Lonnie's end of the scale fell, he knew he had wagered too much. He used to wake up and make coffee when they were on the road. Ev woke up not long after. She'd smile. Sometimes they'd talk, but more often they would watch the sunrise—a luxury that they could afford even in hard times, even without a roof over their heads. It was a little thing, maybe, but the thought of letting it go brought Lonnie nearly to tears.

The man laughed again—a profane sound, even for this horrible place. "Coffee together? How sentimental. I'll put that up too."

The scales equalized.

"I wonder what it will be like to have two memories of the same event," said the man, dealing five cards to each of them. "Maybe it'll be like a stereoscope—greater depth, I mean. Or maybe I'll just go mad."

Lonnie picked up his cards, trying to keep his face blank. Five cards—a pair of nines, the rest useless. A tricky hand. Evelyn would have known what to do. Could he win with a pair of nines? Or should he fold and try again, giving up the memory he had put on the scale? *Could* he give it up—even something as little as that?

No.

He had already lost her once.

One memory had followed Lonnie through ten years of searching— driving him when he grew tired, never allowing him to rest. That memory filled him now, and—almost before he had decided what to do—the scale drew it from his mind.

"It all happened so fast," he said. "We were careless—we had been winning too much that night. Ev was blinking at me, signaling a bad hand, and someone figured it out. I couldn't tell what was happening—there was a loud noise and something on the ground. I thought someone had knocked over a chair. Then he tried to shoot me and I ran. I thought she was behind me."

As he spoke, Lonnie could feel Evelyn's presence behind him, though he didn't dare look. Her sightless eyes burned into the back of his head. Lonnie didn't flinch.

"I remember," said the man. "She saw him draw but didn't have time to react. First bullet in the shoulder, second bullet in the chest. They felt like two sledgehammers. She died in seconds—there was nothing you could have done. Still, the last thing she saw was you running out the door."

The scales balanced.

Lonnie discarded three cards and drew three. The dead man discarded nothing. Two pair—nines and tens. Not great. Not terrible.

Lonnie barely looked at them.

It didn't matter.

He had first met Evelyn across a poker table. She won a fortune from him that day, with an audacious bluff and nothing in her hand. Just determination.

Lonnie had that. Ten years of it. He would never leave Evelyn behind again. He stared into the dead man's shifty, unreadable eyes.

An audacious bluff...

"I'll bet all my memories of her," he said.

Lonnie tried to hold it all in his head at once: the good, the bad, everything in between.

Rich times, with pockets full of stolen money. Poor times, with hardly a piece of stale bread between them. Sitting across the table as opponents— the day she'd first said hello. Sitting across the table as partners—the day she didn't know to say goodbye. The scales took it all.

For a while, neither of them spoke.

Then the man smiled.

"I'll raise," he said. "I bet Evelyn. All her memories—her whole life."

The scales moved again—heavier now on the man's side than Lonnie's.

"You'll have to go all in," he said. "A life for a life. If you win, you'll get her back. If you lose, you'll be a shell like her—stuck on that balcony, forever. Either way, at least you'll be together."

The man leaned back in his chair, and though his eyes swirled with a hundred different emotions, Lonnie thought he could see triumph. It was over. The man had called the bluff. He had probably stacked the deck from the beginning—Lonnie would have watched closer, if he had been thinking straight. He had come so close and none of it mattered. He was about to lose everything.

Unless...

There was another way to finish this. Lonnie knew the way out. He had stood at a crossroads, followed the lonely cry of the jay, slept for a day and a night under a grafted apple tree. He could fold. He would lose the memories of Evelyn—the memories that had dogged his steps for ten long years, that had robbed him of his joy. They were just memories. They weren't her—they were nothing.

He would start again.

Lonnie searched the man for any hint of doubt, hoping against hope that there was another way—but there was nothing. He drew in breath, preparing to say the word that would end his journey. The man just kept blinking at him, incessantly, inhumanly—too much energy, too much life.

Blink.

Blink.

Blink.

And suddenly Lonnie understood. It was Evelyn.

Lonnie had been wrong all along. Evelyn wasn't behind him, accusing him with a blind stare. She had been across the table, just like always. She was part of this man, seeing through his eyes—and she had signaled Lonnie the same way she had on their last day together. The man had nothing in his hand. He was bluffing.

This time Lonnie didn't hesitate.

"Call."

Lonnie threw his cards onto the table, revealing his two pair. The man had stopped blinking, and his face—once so animated—was suddenly very grave. His fingers lost their strength and his cards fell, landing face up on the table.

No pair. Nothing.

Lonnie had won.

Suddenly Lonnie's mind was swimming with memories—most of them familiar, yet slightly different. Days and nights together. Moments he had treasured and moments he hadn't realized he had forgotten. He could have spent days standing completely still—holding it all in, understanding her completely—but he could feel each memory tugging away from him, drawn toward Evelyn like iron filings drawn toward a magnet. He let them go.

And Evelyn woke up.

She smiled. It was the same smile that Lonnie remembered. The one he never thought he would see again. He could hardly believe it.

"I was worried you couldn't see me," she said.

Lonnie couldn't keep the tears from his eyes.

Evelyn climbed down from the balcony, and they held each other for a long time. Then, hand in hand, they walked out the batwing doors of Gambler's Rest—away from the horrible man, the dead faces, the despair. She was very pale, but color returned to her cheeks with every step—a little farther, and two lead bullets fell gently into the snow—farther still, her wounds knitted and she began to shiver. Lonnie could see her breath. He gave her his coat.

It was hard to see through the swirling snow, but the sun had just begun to rise.

About the Author

Joshua Boers lives in Grand Rapids, Michigan. He has contributed short stories and poetry to *Infinity Wanderers* and *The MockingOwl Roost*. By day, he is an editorial assistant at an independent book publisher. By night, he can generally be found reading P. G. Wodehouse novels, playing with his cat Mishka or writing sonnets based on randomly selected Wikipedia articles.

Adult Judges' Choice Runner-Up

The Hemlock House
Kelly Selby

The cabin that's meant to save me comes into view. Its A-frame barely peeks out from the hemlocks to greet us. Without the GPS, we would have driven right past it. I step onto the porch while Nelson unloads our luggage. The cedar shingles are worn with age but give the home the coziness that I hoped for.

"Things will be better here. I know it," Nelson says as he joins me.

I nod a response.

A wooden sign above the entry reads *The Hemlock House*. The deep grooves of the letters are painted a bright red that match the door. We find the key the host left for us and step inside. We can take in the entire cabin without going further than the doormat. Above us is a loft that holds the only bedroom. The A-framed roof limits the ceiling space, making it a tight fit for two adults. The cabin itself will be a tight fit for us. Our own house isn't what I would consider large, but it's certainly spacious enough. Although lately it's felt like too much separation.

I pull my laptop from my bag and set it on the small desk by the window, where I'll spend most of my waking hours for the next several months. My writing has been stagnant. I've been freelancing for several magazines and running my blog for over five years. I keep promising myself I'll start a novel, but I break that promise each day.

The inadequacy I felt had been getting to me, so when Nelson suggested renting a cabin to escape, I agreed. Despite feeling cliché, I was desperate and wanted to stop the concern that etched his face more and more each day. He worries it will happen again. I worry too, just not about that. Instead, I fret about my career. About him. About us. The additional workload placed on Nelson's shoulders after his recent promotion is a strain felt throughout our home.

"Amber, come look."

I join Nelson at the back of the cabin, where he looks out the floor to ceiling windows at a river winding through the woods.

"You didn't mention we would be on a river," I say.

Nelson shrugs. "It wasn't mentioned on the booking site. Want to go check it out?" "Sure."

We step outside and I feel the cold air rolling in as the sun starts to drop.

It's still early fall, but we're farther north than I'm used to. We make the short walk down. The wide river surges against the banks and cascades over rocks.

As I take a step forward, my foot slips on a wet rock. I lose my balance and brace myself for the fall. Thankfully, I feel Nelson's hand grab hold of my arm before I do.

"Careful there. We don't want you falling in. At least not on our first night," he teases. I laugh as a chill runs up my back and I wrap my sweater tighter around me.

***

The next morning, I descend the ladder quietly, trying not to wake Nelson. I brew a pot of coffee, grateful that the cabin has a full sized coffee maker, and sit down at the desk, determined to start writing. After two cups of coffee, a blank page still stares up at me.

"Morning, darling," Nelson says as he makes his way down a few hours later.

"Perfect timing." I shut my laptop. "I was just going to go for a walk if you'd like to join me?"

"Already needing a break from your book?" He winks.

I smile but don't reply, not wanting to admit I hadn't even written a word yet. Grabbing a sweater off the back of my chair, I follow after him down the driveway that weaves through the trees.

"Seriously though, how's the book going?"

"It's… going. It's a slow start, but I think being here will help."

"Sometimes the hardest thing with anything is just getting started. You're going to do great. Don't worry." He pulls me in and gives me a kiss on the top of the head. "How are you feeling?"

My cheeks flush. He's always waiting for me to crack. "Good." I clear my throat. "So, are you going to survive without working in the office?"

"Most of our staff are still working from home, so they'll survive without me being in for a bit. Plus, I've been in the office enough lately."

He's not wrong. Nelson has been in so much after his promotion that I barely see him. You'd think it would give me more time to write, but I feel lonely and even more unproductive in his absence.

Back in the cabin, I sit down once more in front of a blank screen.

It's not that I don't have ideas, I just don't know if any are novel worthy.

A book is a commitment. One I don't take lightly.

After a few hours of procrastinating by working on a blog post, I lay down for a nap knowing I don't deserve one, yet still wanting one anyway. When I wake up, the cabin is empty and I head down to the river for some fresh air. I stand along the wide bank, hugging my arms as the breeze picks up.

Suddenly, hands are against my back. Before I can comprehend what's happening, I'm falling. The cold water is a shock to my body and I fight to stay afloat. My feet search for the river bed and come up short. My head breaks free of the water and I can finally catch my breath. As I do, I make out the figure standing along the bank.

Nelson.

This can't be happening. Why would he do this? How could he do this? My mind fights to comprehend it, while my body struggles even more. My arms thrash and grab hold of something soft. A blanket. I come to on the couch. It was just a dream. A very real dream. My hands shake as I try to steady myself to sit up.

Tea. That will help calm my nerves. My hands still tremble as I fill a kettle with water. The image of Nelson standing along the river bank flashes in my mind and I almost drop it. I try to search for a meaning while waiting for the water to boil but give up.

As I sip the tea, my shoulders relax. I feel foolish for reacting so strongly to a dream. People have nightmares all the time. There's no need for me to overreact. The stress has been getting to me, which could certainly cause issues with sleep. I tell myself that's all it is—that it's not happening again—and make a mental note to start my meditation practice back up.

The front door swings open and Nelson steps through, drenched in sweat. I'm glad he was out during my nightmare.

"How was your run?" I ask.

"It was great! Did you know there's a trail just down the road? And I had it all to myself. There must not be many other cabins in this area."

"That's great, hon. I'll have to check it out."

I get up and dig through the fridge for something to make for dinner, the dream already fading from memory. We haven't packed as many groceries as I thought and we'll need to go into town soon, although I'm not actually sure where that would be. We hadn't passed any towns for a long time before we reached the cabin. I'm normally the one who books our trips, but this time Nelson offered to make the reservation.

***

The next morning, I bring my laptop to the front porch so I won't disturb Nelson during his meeting. A thin layer of frost covers the grass, reminding me that we're inching closer to winter. Instead of writing, I search for the nearest town, which ends up being almost fifteen miles away. Hopefully, we won't have to make too many trips there.

I check the time and know his meeting will just be ending, so I step back into the cabin. He slams his laptop screen down as I do. He sits with his eyes closed and earphones still in as he takes in several deep breaths.

"Everything okay?" I ask.

He opens his eyes and tugs the earpieces out. "Yes, everything's fine."

My gaze doesn't leave his, hoping he'll say more, but he gets up and leaves out the back door.

I've gotten used to Nelson being evasive about some aspects of his life. It used to bother me when we first started dating. He was married previously and I know almost nothing about her. When I try to press for information, I'm always met with resistance. I don't try anymore. I've accepted that there are some people who are an open book and others who wouldn't let you pry that book open for anything. Nelson is the latter. I made peace with that before we married. However, it would be nice to be able to flip through his pages occasionally.

***

Two days later, the dream happens again. This time Nelson holds me down while I scream and try to kick my way free from the water. The last thing I remember before waking is looking into his pale blue eyes.

Then I'm on the couch drenched in sweat as if I had been in the river.

Nelson appears in front of me and I startle. I thought he was out for a run.

His lips are pursed as he sits down next to me. "Are you okay?"

My heart pounds in my chest. "Yeah, I'm fine."

His hazel eyes look at me with concern. Why did I dream that he had blue eyes? Why am I having these dreams at all?

"All this stress and pressure you're putting on yourself to write this book." His hand moves to rub my back. "Do you think you should call Dr. Porter?"

I shake my head and stand up from the couch. "No. I'm just a little stressed, but I'm fine." I hate the way he's looking at me. "Seriously, this isn't like before." But did I know that? He nods. "Okay."

I push those thoughts away and sit down at my desk, determined to write something. Anything. The words start spilling out of me. I write about a couple who rents a cabin for their honeymoon. Normally I have trouble naming my characters, but theirs come right to me. Irene and Joel.

It's as if Nelson and I are playing out their lives within my dreams. Nelson is impressed at my sudden speed as I type away until the sun sets each day. I haven't told him about my unexpected inspiration for the story.

Nelson walks up behind me now as I'm typing and his hands rub my shoulders. "Want to call it a night and join me by the fire?"

I tell him just fifteen more minutes. He sighs and heads to the kitchen, where I hear the clink of ice as he pours himself a drink. Then I write about Joel pouring himself one and can feel Irene's nervous energy. He always drinks more than she prefers. It's getting worse and so is his anger.

With each new sentence, I feel tension and fear building in my body. My shoulders are up to my ears. I hit the save button and decide to take Nelson up on his offer.

***

The following afternoon, I'm on the couch after my latest nightmare. Dr. Porter's contact stares up at me from my phone as my thumb hovers over the call option. They're just dreams, I tell myself—this isn't a break in my reality—people have dreams all the time. Plus, I don't actually want them to end, do I? They're terrifying, but they're also inspiring.

I toss my phone on the couch and return to my desk where I complete another few thousands words all before dinnertime.

"Amber?"

I jump and turn to see Nelson standing beside me. His arms are folded across his chest. "I've been calling your name. Did you not hear me?"

"Sorry, got lost in the story, I guess."

His brows furrow just slightly. "Okay. Well, I was trying to tell you dinners ready. It's a little warmer tonight, so I thought we could eat on the back porch?"

My eyes slide past him and to the river. It's foolish, but I'm still nervous about going near the water. "Sure."

I follow him outside, where he's already set the tiny patio table for our meal. A small candle sits lit between our plates. I wonder if that was already in the cabin or if he thought to pack it.

"So, are you going to tell me what the book is about yet?"

A piece of fish lodges in my throat and I swallow it down. "Not yet. I'd like to work through the entire plot first." I've always shared my story ideas with him, but this one I want to hold back.

His eyes stay on me for a few moments before he nods in understanding.

We're both quiet, and I can hear the water rushing its way through the woods. It's a sound most find relaxing, but it causes me to go cold. Or maybe it's just the evening chill setting in. I look over at Nelson and force a smile.

***

The past week, I've taken to driving the fifteen miles to town in order to write in their small coffee shop. Away from Nelson. It's foolish, I know, but as the dreams and my story continue, the lines between Nelson and Joel blur. I find myself typing Nelson's name instead of Joel's and once I almost called him Joel to his face.

The only problem with the cafe is that I seem to have lost all inspiration. It's as if the only time the story comes to me is when I'm in the cabin. I close my eyes and try to envision its moss covered cedar siding. The wooden interior. The worn top of my tiny desk. When I open my eyes, the words still don't come to me.

My phone buzzes on the table and I read the text from Nelson asking when I'll be back. I let out a sigh and pack up my things. The sooner I write this draft, the sooner I can go home. Back to where I feel safe.

When I get back to the cabin, Nelson is nowhere to be found. It's odd, but I don't mind. I quickly get back to work like a bee returning to its hive.

I'm nearing the end of the story and it's almost too difficult to write. Tears well in my eyes as I type about Irene hiding from Joel.

Suddenly I hear a scream. My head whips behind me, trying to find the source. It sounded as if it came from the river. I hesitate for a moment before running out the back door. I search through the woods, but find nothing.

As I turn to head back to the cabin, I collide with Nelson.

"What are you doing out here?" he asks.

My breath is choppy. "I thought I heard something."

His gaze studies me, and I move to walk away before he replies. He grabs hold of my arm. I struggle under his grip as he drags me closer to the river's edge. This has to be another dream. This can't actually be happening.

I feel the shock of cold water in my bones as I plead with him to let me go. "Please," I call out one last time as I sink below the surface.

Tears stream down my face as I come to in the loft. My whole body is shaking. This has to stop, I tell myself. I descend the ladder swiftly, slipping on the last rung. My hands type even quicker as I finish Irene's story.

Once I'm done, I feel a weight lift off my shoulders.

After I save the draft, I pack up my laptop and the rest of my belongings. When Nelson returns, I'm going to demand we go. I need to be home. Away from this cabin. From these nightmares.

***

Over two years—and many drafts later—my book has been published. It's been out for a week and the reviews have been mostly positive.

Tonight, Nelson and I will celebrate our three-year wedding anniversary.

This should be the happiest time of my life. Instead, I'm pacing my office with a pit in my stomach.

The evening before I had received an email with only one line included, "How could you use my daughter's memory like this?" After a quick internet search of Irene and the city in Michigan where the cabin was located, I found an article that was published five years before. It covered a story about a woman named Irene from Indiana who had tragically drowned in the river while on her honeymoon. Included was a photo of the young couple beaming and in love. I never saw their faces in my dreams, but I'll never forget those eyes.

The article makes no mention of foul play, and I'm sure any other reader would be thinking about this poor widowed husband. But not me. I feel angry. Anger that he could get away with this. Anger that he's smiling up at the readers from their wedding photo, fooling everyone.

I jump as there's a knock at the door. Our delivery drivers alway knock for us after dropping off a package. I swing open the door, expecting to scoop up a box from the mat. Instead, a man with pale blue eyes stands there. Before I have time to think, I slam the door in his face—although not fast enough. He catches it with his foot and pulls it open.

"Joel?" I ask, already knowing the answer.

About the Author

Kelly Selby is a graduate of Michigan State University and lives in mid-Michigan with her husband and dog. She works in IT by day and writes fiction by night. In her free time, she enjoys running and biking the trails and attending trivia nights with her family.

Adult Readers' Choice Winner

Home
Samantha Engel

Something tore Claire from her sleep. A creeping sense of unease swirled in her stomach as she blinked her eyes into focus. The full moon lit up her room, allowing her to see that nothing appeared out of place.

Even Duncan laid in his usual spot on the floor next to her bed, his paws twitching from the dream playing in his head.

She let out a deep breath and whispered, "Everything is fine."

As Claire snuggled back down into bed, she looked out the window across from her and considered the differences between this view of moonlit trees and that of the city apartment she had left. Just as her eyelids began drooping with sleep, movement outside caught her attention.

A figure stepped out from behind a tree and walked into view. Claire gasped and shot up. She crawled to the end of her bed to gain a better view and spotted the large figure moving toward the woods. Duncan stirred and began pacing around the room nervously, while Claire watched the figure disappear into the tree line. An eerie whooping noise echoed from the woods and Duncan began whining.

"Duncan, here," Claire whispered and patted the bed. The dog jumped up and together they both watched and waited.

Several minutes passed and, with no sign of the prowler, Claire looked at Duncan and said, "We should probably get back to sleep."

Duncan replied with a strange, almost conversational noise before spinning around in three circles and laying on the bed. "Yes, you should stay up here to protect me," Claire whispered and closed her eyes.

Sleep eluded Claire for the rest of the night, though. She watched as the minutes inched closer to her 6:30 alarm until she finally gave up at 6:00. It was Thursday, so she needed to get up to make the 40-minute drive from her home in Munising to Marquette, where she taught English at Northern Michigan University. She drug herself out of bed and made her way through her morning routine. Some days, Claire's long commute to work allowed her to unplug or think through her projects, but the previous night's ordeal caused doubt to creep into her mind. She recalled the incredulous looks on her parents' faces when she told them she was moving to the Upper

Peninsula and remembered the skepticism that laced her friends' questions.

Even the realtor looked shocked when Claire told him she'd be moving to Munising alone. The memories weighed heavy on her.

"Maybe I can't do this," she choked out. Tears threatened to spill out of her eyes, but she blinked them away and forced herself to remember what got her to this point.

"You, Owen! You're my problem!" Claire yelled as tears fell from her eyes. "You are never here. Even when you're here," she motioned around the room," you're not here, with me."

"Where is this coming from?" Owen asked, his eyes wide.

"From all of the times I said that we need to spend time together and then you wrapped yourself up in something of your own instead, and when you can't even take meat out of the freezer when you work from home.

We don't even talk before bed." Claire's voice had grown quiet by the final sentence. "How can you not see the problems?"

"I guess I don't."

"Then that's how oblivious you are, Owen. I have been miserable for a long time. I tried talking, but you couldn't be bothered to listen."

"What are you saying?"

"That if you aren't even willing to engage in a conversation about how I feel, it's over."

"What is there to talk about?"

Claire stared at him. She moved from anger to shock to resolve in a matter of seconds.

"Goodbye, Owen," Claire whispered and took the dishcloth she had been using to dry dishes off of her shoulder. She slowly walked to the bedroom and began packing a suitcase.

"Are you serious?"

"I'm not staying here tonight. If you want to talk about it, you can call me tomorrow," she said to him. "Otherwise, I'll be back tomorrow evening to get the rest of my things."

"Where are you going?"

"Rachel's," she said, referring to a colleague she knew would let her stay the night.

Claire called Duncan and together they left without another word. Owen never called.

Claire often replayed this fight when she needed a boost of courage. The growing disinterest from her partner of six years had reached a breaking point and she knew that she needed to start again. A perfect storm of events had come together after she moved back in with her parents in Grand

Rapids; she'd found a tenure track job teaching at Northern, a small house with property in Munising, and she decided to make the move.

The stretch of state highway Claire drove to Marquette was lined with little scenic pull-offs and roadside parks, all with beautiful beaches and views of Lake Superior. As she approached her favorite spot, Claire decided she could spare a few minutes to walk down to the lake and clear her mind.

She parked her car under a maple tree which had turned bright orange and walked past the small picnic area, through the sandy beach grass, and across the stoney shore to the water's edge. She slipped out of her flats and put the tips of her toes in the glassy, cold water as the wind, which rarely stopped along the shore, whipped her hair around her. Claire took in a deep breath of the lake air.

The smell brought back childhood memories of summer afternoons spent at her grandparents' cabin on the lake. Her grandfather told her stories about shipwrecks, local legends, and wildlife encounters from his own childhoods spent up here with his parents, as she hunted for pretty stones. She could almost taste the campfire bacon, wild-berry pies, and hot chocolate that her grandmother made.

Even as a child, Claire felt called to the lake. When she left at the end of the summer, it always felt like she was breaking off a piece of herself as she watched Lake Superior disappear behind them. Others thought she was insane when she moved up here, but it felt right in her heart. After staring out over the endless expanse of water for a few more moments, Claire slipped back into her shoes, her toes almost frozen, and headed back up to her car. As she resumed her journey to work, a sense of calm washed away the terror she felt about the incident the previous night, but an unease still persisted.

Claire decided to play it safe for the next couple of weeks and didn't go out after dark.

When she ran errands around town, Duncan typically accompanied her and the Munising residents got used to seeing him in the passenger's seat. She wanted everyone to know she wasn't alone in the woods. As Claire became further removed from the strange sighting, though, she thought of several rational explanations that did not include criminal activity.

"Perhaps," she told Duncan one day, "a hunter from the Lower Peninsula had found himself lost or" she continued, "a neighbor didn't know anyone had bought this property yet."

After a month, Claire had largely pushed the visitor out of her mind.

One morning, as she drank her coffee on the front porch she casually said, "I think we could probably run again," and looked down at her canine companion. Duncan immediately picked up his head and began thumping his tail against the wooden deck. Claire had been taking Duncan for regular runs since he was two and they both found the quiet of the seasonal roads and trails near the house far more peaceful and enjoyable than city sidewalks or a busy park. If Claire was going to live here, she thought, she needed to be comfortable with the solitude, instead of letting it limit her.

She stood up, and Duncan began circling her as she walked into the house to change for the run.

The rhythmic slap of Claire's feet on the packed dirt of the seasonal road could be heard throughout the surrounding pine woods. She worked to steady her breath and turned the volume of her music up to drown out the sound of her breathing. Duncan ran next to Claire with a running leash attached to her waist. To their left, the pine forest began at the edge of the road, but to their right, a wide strip of scrubby grass sat between the road and the forest, along which a row of electric towers hummed.

Claire glanced down at Duncan and smiled, as he matched her step for step. When she looked back to the road, she saw something that caused her to stop in her tracks. A large, bulky figure stood in the middle of the road about fifty feet in front of them. Claire shielded her eyes from the sun and, although she could only make out a shadow, she was sure it had a shaggy or hairy outline.

"Hello?" Claire called as she removed her earbuds. Duncan issued a low, warning growl and the hair on his back stood up, as he bared his teeth in the direction of the shadow.

The hulking figure stood silent.

"Do you need something?" she asked.

A few more beats of silence passed before a loud, animalistic whooping sound came from the woods to Claire's left, causing her to jump and Duncan began barking. A hollow sound, like two pieces of wood slapping together, echoed through the forest, and the figure in the road darted toward the tree line as if being called back. Claire stood frozen in place and her rapid heartbeat echoed in her ears.

"Come on, boy," she urgently whispered to Duncan after she regained her bearings.

Claire wiped the tears from her eyes as the pair turned to walk home.

The return took longer than Claire would've liked, but she couldn't muster the coordination or control of breath to run. Claire's muscles eased as her cabin came into view and she felt the pull of its safety welcoming her home. She and Duncan hurried up the porch steps and, once inside, she locked the screen and interior doors. Before unhooking Duncan from his running lead, Claire stepped into the kitchen and splashed water from the sink on her face. She then filled a glass and slid down to the floor with her back against the cupboards.

"This was the worst idea. I'm an idiot," she said aloud as the tears fell freely from her eyes. As she cried, Duncan laid down between Claire and the door, but left his head up and alert.

Claire set her water aside and leaned over on top of him. She gave in to the fear and worry and let the doubts take hold as she cried into his fur.

Eventually, the tears ended and Claire sat up. She wiped her eyes and let out a few deep, meditative breaths to calm herself. As she did, a strange thought crossed her mind. Her folklorist brain began working and with a new, academic zeal, she hurried to her office and searched her bookshelf for anything vaguely connected to wild men, creatures from Great Lakes folklore, and unexplained mysteries. Once she had amassed a respectable pile on her desk, she turned on her computer and her fingers hesitated over the keyboard. *Am I really about to do this?* Claire closed her eyes and, without looking, she typed "Upper Peninsula Bigfoot" into the search bar.

A variety of news articles appeared with stories of individuals claiming to have seen the famous cryptozoological creature. Claire noted the similarities between these accounts and her own encounters. Reports of whoops, knocks, and large imposing figures sent a familiar shiver down her spine. She turned to her books and found legends of wild men, hairy monsters, and Sasquatch in a variety of cultures across the globe.

Just after 11:00, Claire sat back in her chair and let out a frustrated howl. Duncan ran into her office and placed his head in her lap. He raised his dark eyebrows to look at her.

"I'm going crazy," she said as she met his gaze. "You might as well pack up your Milkbones and find a normal mom." At that, the dog whined and Claire laughed in response. She gave him a final ear scratch before standing and making her way to the shower.

As the water hit her body, Claire shook out her limbs, as though she were wiggling out the morning's experience and the complex thoughts now floating through her head. *Am I the kind of person who believes in this stuff?*

As she considered these possibilities, Claire yearned for the comfort of her family.

Claire taught afternoon classes on Wednesdays, which allowed the noon sun to warm her through the windshield as she pulled onto the highway toward Marquette. Explanations and possibilities swam through her mind, despite her best efforts to distract herself with music and, when that failed, a new audiobook. Claire soon felt an all-too-familiar panic begin to take hold.

Her heart raced and her hands felt clammy. It became difficult to focus on the road as a light-headed feeling overcame her. To Claire's relief, she saw her scenic park ahead and turned off the highway.

After parking in the empty lot, Claire fought to open her car door and then stumbled over the stone covered path down to the beach. Her chest ached as her breathing came in rapid, shallow gasps. The logical part of her brain told her to call 911, but something deeper pulled her to Superior.

She stepped into the icy, late-fall water and the shock of the cold stole her ragged breaths. A squeal escaped her lips, and, when she took her next inhalation, it was deep and filled her lungs.

Claire closed her eyes and inhaled a few more deep, meditative breaths. Then, she slowly opened them and took in the familiar view around her. All of the deciduous trees had lost their leaves now, but the scraggly conifers that filled the Upper Peninsula's landscape kept it from looking barren.

The sky was November gray and looked like it could spit rain, or even snow, at any moment, but the water was unusually calm. As Claire thought back to her grandparents, a sudden splash in front of her broke her concentration. She couldn't see any cause for the ripples in the perfectly clear water, so Claire turned around and her heart began to race once again.

Near the shore, a few yards east of the beach, stood a large figure similar to the one she had seen that morning. This time, though, without sun and shadows, she could clearly see the bulky, hairy, primate-like figure that had been lurking in the back of her mind since that first night.

Did it throw something at me? Her mind told her to act rationally and run, but this time Claire wasn't afraid. In this place, which had been a part of her for decades, Claire listened to her heart. It had guided her to this moment; from the break-up, to the move, and now to the water.

Claire began taking slow, steady steps toward the creature and it gave no indication of harming her. As she crept closer, she began to make out more details, like its relaxed fingers, loose shoulders and, finally, its soft, brown eyes. As though broken out of a trance, Claire jumped when she suddenly realized her feet had carried her within five feet of the creature. He flinched, but didn't take a step.

"Were you trying to tell me something?" she asked softly and took a few more steps.

The being extended a hand toward Claire and she held hers out to it. Its large, dark brown hands cupped her own and Claire felt calm for the first time in a long time. The creature took a small step forward and cupped the side of her face in its hand. His skin felt soft and warm against her cheek.

Then, she watched as the corners of his mouth turned up to smile and he nodded at Claire. He used his thumb to brush away a tear that had fallen from her eye before letting her go, turning, and walking away in the forest.

More tears welled up in Claire's eyes as she processed what had happened. *It's not trying to hurt me,* Claire thought as she watched the creature disappear into the forest. *It's been watching over me.* She sniffled and cleared her throat before heading back up to her car with a new confidence; she had made the right decision to move here. The mysteries that had pulled her to this desolate, sometimes-harsh, environment were the ones that would comfort and protect her.

She was home.

About the Author

Samantha Engel grew up in the woods of West Michigan but has lived in Saginaw County for the past ten years. Although she has spent most of this decade using her master's degree in American history in the museum field, she has dreamed of writing fiction since grade school. Samantha finds inspiration in Michigan's landscape and the stories of its past, and believes in the grounding power of place. She also wants her writing to challenge people to wonder what would happen if the folktales and ghost stories we dismissed as children really did exist.

Adult Published Finalist

11:27pm

Nathan Grajek

The following story contains themes of suicide and may be distressing to some readers. If you or someone you know is struggling with thoughts of suicide, please reach out to a mental health professional or contact the Suicide and Crisis Lifeline at 988 for support.

It's 11:27pm

You lay in bed. You are too tired to sleep after being in bed since you got home.

It's 6:40am

You hear your alarm in another dimension. You do not wake up.

It's 7:22am

You send a message to your boss saying you are sick and cannot come to work today.

It's 10:43am

You make it out of bed and into the shower. You turn the water on. You sit on the shower floor because standing is too much.

It's 11:09am

You feel the water is getting cold but you can't move.

It's 11:11am

The freezing water shocks you into turning it off and wrapping in a towel. It's nice to feel something.

It's 12:14pm

You open the refrigerator and consider eating. Instead you sit down and look at your phone.

It's 3:55pm

You are still looking at your phone. The social app asks you if you remember a picture of yourself from 8 years ago when you were smiling. The left corner of your mouth raises slightly as you try to remember what it was like to be happy.

It's 3:56pm

You put the phone down and now look at nothing instead.

It's 6:41pm

You go to your closet and open the door. You look up at the top shelf. It's 6:42pm

You close the closet door and walk away.

It's 6:45pm

You open the closet door again and grab the dark case from the top shelf and hold it. You return the case and close the closet door.

It's 6:59pm

You sit down and start to write a letter.

It's 7:06pm

You rip the letter apart and throw the pieces away.

It's 7:09pm

You retrieve the ripped apart letter from the trash and rip it into smaller pieces before flushing them down the toilet.

It's 7:20pm

You eat, then go to bed.

It's 6:40am

You wake up to your alarm.

It's 7:48am

You are racing down the road to get to work. You want to think about what it would be like if you slid into oncoming traffic and died but you don't think about that.

It's 8:01am

Everything at work is gray. You pretend it has color. You are very good at pretending.

It's 2:27pm

You forget to pretend for a moment and everything becomes too real to handle. You begin to cry. It's 2:31pm

You finally manage to stop crying and go back to pretending. No one noticed you crying, at least no one let you know they noticed.

You are gray, the world is gray, so you blend in fine and remember that no one would care if you stopped being.

It's 5:17pm

You go back to your closet, open the door, take out the case and look at it. It is dark and heavy. You set it in front of you and your thumbs glide across the latch. Your phone vibrates. You push the case away. You do not check your phone.

It's 5:58pm

You have stopped crying. Your phone vibrates. You look at it, but do nothing else. You go to bed. It's 10:59pm

You wake up from a sleeping nightmare that was based on a real nightmare you survived years ago. This is common.

Your entire body is in pain. This is constant.

It's 11:16pm

You go back to the heavy dark case and sit before it.

It's 11:12pm

You open the case and hold the gun in your hands.

It's 11:26pm

You place the end of the barrel of the gun against your skull and take a deep breath.

It's 11:27pm

Tears fall from your eyes as you pull the trigger.

About the Author

Nathan Grajek is a father, husband and social worker living in Battle Creek, MI, where he works as a psychotherapist. He enjoys serving in the community and at his kids' schools. For Nathan, writing is a creative outlet, but his favorite hobby is playing and running tabletop games such as Dungeons and Dragons.

Adult Published Finalist

My Sister's Promise
Heather Picardat

Dear Ayla,

Happy birthday sweet baby sister. How I wish I was there to celebrate with you. Instead, I'm sending along a gift. Remember when I told you that I had something very important to share with you when you were older?

You're older now. I tried to call, but I was choking on the words, and I don't want to break that promise. So I hope this letter finds you well and maybe someday we can talk about it face to face.

I was fifteen, just like you are now. And much like I'm sure you do, I was staying up incredibly late every single night. We didn't have Tik-Tok back then, but we had Youtube and instant messenger, which were both equally as addictive. I used to stay up until 3 or 4 in the morning sometimes. Often, I would skip first period altogether, because I stupidly stayed up way too late, talking to friends on the internet. Don't do that by the way. Education is very important.

Anyway, you were a baby, maybe 6 months old at this time and it was a Monday night. I remember because I had marching band rehearsal that night.

I came home, immediately took a shower, put on my pajamas (an oversized Bugs Bunny shirt with no pants) and then I holed up in my room for the night.

I liked to just sit in the dark sometimes, snuggled up in a blanket and just get lost on the computer. Minutes would creep into hours and before I knew it, all the commotion of regular family cacophony had faded away. As far as I knew I was the only one still awake. Midnight came and went, then 1 o'clock, but as 2am was approaching, I began hearing footsteps outside of my door. I knew I would have been in trouble if Mom knew I was still awake, so quickly I switched the computer monitor off. I bundled up in my comforter and I jumped into bed, laying on my side so that my head was turned opposite the door.

The door creaked open; there was a moment of silence. Several moments later, The distinct sound of bare feet on carpet made its way closer and closer to my bed. I laid as still as I could, feigning a believable sleep. Up until this point, I had believed that it was Mom who was in my room. I had believed that she was revving up her lecture, after having seen the light from my computer monitor from underneath the door. I had assumed that I woke little baby you up and that that was the problem. All of these guesses were far from reality. As someone sat on my bed, I heard the distinct sound of your dad whispering, though rather loudly, "Can I sleep in here tonight?"

My eyes shot open. But I laid in disbelief for a moment until he repeated himself. "I just want to sleep with you tonight." He said. I turned my body slightly, to indicate to him that I was trying to sleep, but I was frozen with anxiety. I couldn't make my voice say anything. The moment he saw my eyes, his face morphed into a horrific smile that I had never seen before.

A little louder this time, as he wrapped his arms around me, turning me to face him, he then whispered to me, "Where's the beef? I can show you."

His hands were searching my body, touching surfaces that had never been touched by anyone before. I wanted to scream, I wanted to call out.

I wanted Mom to come into my room, scoop me up and help me feel safe. But I didn't.

There's a thousand things that people wish they would do in situations like this, things they think they would do. You could claim all day long that you would have screamed if you were me, but I think you'd be just as shocked as I would to learn how your body actually forces you to react.

Mine made me feel like I was in quicksand, like my body was detached from my brain, like my muscles were jello and my voice was absent. No matter how hard I tried, I couldn't make my mouth form any words loud enough to reach across my bedroom floor.

He laid there spooning me for a moment, hand cupping my breast, as I lay lifelessly, just silently coping with the situation. Something must have clicked, like he didn't know it was my room he was in, and he urgently stood after several minutes. He quickly walked out the door, closing it behind him.

Moments later, I heard the bedroom door across the hall shut, followed by a faint cry, yours.

I was in a full panic. After I determined that I truly was the last one awake, and I knew there was no way I was going to get to sleep, I cradled myself, gently crying in the corner of my room. It had to have been close to 3am at this point. I called the only person I thought I could trust.

"Bette, are you awake?"

"Barely"

"I really need you. I'm sorry it's so late."

"What do you need?"

"Can your mom take me to the police? Please, I can't sleep here tonight."

About 30 minutes passed, and I was sneaking out my window, into Aunt Myrah's car. I cried the entire way to the police station. Aunt Myrah asked me every question she could think of, and I answered them all the best I could. I had felt completely violated, like my innocence was ripped from me and all I did was lay there. When we arrived at the police station, I was seen almost immediately. I told this story to a female cop, and then a male cop and then another female, over and over again, just repeating what had happened.

The third cop made me reiterate everything I said at least 3 times, after which she finally said to me, " Are we pressing charges or not?" I was so exhausted.

I had been up all day and now all night, I was a teenager with no grasp on what rights I had, what pressing charges would mean. All I kept thinking was Mom is going to freak if the baby wakes up right now. I didn't know what to do, but I knew I would not feel safe going home.

Aunt Myrah saw my discomfort, and offered to just take me home. The police officers talked to her alone for a few minutes and then we were back in the car.

"Please don't take me home." I said, a thousand horrible thoughts swirling in my head. "I won't" she replied and proceeded to drive me to her house.

I slept in Bette's room with her that night. She held me as I cried into her pillows, a welcome form of affection from a trusted cousin. It was incredibly early in the morning when I finally dozed off. I remember watching the sun rise, feeling completely defeated before my body gave in. The adrenaline had given in and now I needed to rest. Aunt Myrah and Bette took the day off to be with me. Aunt Myrah must have let Mom know that I was at her house, but I don't know when she did. All I knew was that Mom decided to go to work anyway and that she was mad at me for sneaking out and not coming home. I barely ate at all that day, but after dinner, Aunt Myrah said that Mom wanted me back home because CPS had showed up and I was supposed to give them a statement.

I could feel the knots building in my throat, making me sick to my stomach.

I knew your Dad would be there, and I knew he would have some kind of smug remark about what he had done to me the night before. I knew Mom would be mad at me for having to deal with CPS, but I also knew I had to go back. I had to interview with CPS and face Mom, no matter how difficult it was to disclose the details that had me so shook up.

When I walked in, the worker was already speaking with Mom and your

Dad. He was cracking jokes with her. There was laughter and then I will never forget what his mouth uttered.

"I'm not attracted to children. She's messed up. She's 15, why would I even be in her room? I wouldn't be. Look, I had some bad weed. Evidently I was more ill than I thought, but I'm not attracted to my wife's daughter."

It's like I was expecting him to deny it,but I wasn't expecting for it to be so out there. She's messed up? I wasn't. True, I was upset. I was completely broken and I didn't know how to handle the situation, but prior to my late night encounter, I wasn't messed up at all. I walked into my room, feeling very confused, as they finished their conversation. My head was pounding.

Did I dream this up? Am I losing my mind? No. There's no way. I flipped on the monitor, my messenger window still open to a conversation I was keeping the night before. I remember feeling a sense of relief in seeing exactly what I remembered doing last. However, that feeling was quickly subdued as I turned to face my bed, to see a red velvet robe tie, lying across my unmade bed.

I swung my door open wide, gasping for air. At the same time, who do I see, walking from the kitchen nook to the living room? Wearing his favorite red velvet robe,tied shut with a leather belt, drink in his hand as he smiles at the CPS worker and says, "Apparently, she needed a little more attention. Sometimes it's like that with a new baby." I look on in horror, as tears well up in my eyes.

Mom and the worker stand, shaking hands. Mom opens the door for her and sees her out. The worker says she will set up an interview for me at school.

She recommends that a psych evaluation is performed for me, and then she says her goodbyes.

"Now we can get on with the night, eh? Hey Hera, thanks for the excitement." your Dad says, winking in my direction. Stunned, frozen in place and altogether defeated, I returned to my room. I pushed the dresser against the door and just sat there, feeling isolated. In the morning, I got up early to talk to Mom, but it was clear she wasn't going to listen. "I know you don't like him, but lying about something like that is really messed up. If he did something to you, why wouldn't you have screamed." I don't know. I still don't know. She wanted to know what made him stop. I don't know.

She wanted to know all the same things I wanted to know.

"Well it's not like he slept with you so I don't see what the big deal is. Whatever this is, is done. It's over so we can move on with our lives"

That was a pivotal moment for me. That's when it was clear that in Mom's eyes, breaching sexual boundaries only happens when there is penetration.

Nevermind that I could feel his entire body against mine. Nevermind that he was intentionally feeling mine. Nevermind that he came in there on his own will, even leaving behind the tie to his robe. How did it get there if he wasn't in there?

I had been violated. My trust, my privacy, my psyche had all been taken advantage of and I had almost nobody in my corner. At some point, Mom contacted the whole family to let them know that anything I disclosed to them about your Dad touching me, was a lie and that I was just craving attention. They all believed her, every single one of them. That Thanksgiving was the beginning of an era for me. Everybody whispered as I entered or exited a room, Grandma looking at me with disappointment; my relationship with every one of them was scarred from that day on.

After Thanksgiving dinner that year, I remember scooping you up into my arms.I promised you I would protect you for as long as I could.

I promised you he would never get to hurt you. The following month, we abruptly uprooted. Mom had packed the entire house, all my things included and announced that we would be moving to North Carolina. I barely had time to say goodbye to my friends. I finished high school, in the same house with you. I started college, still by your side,still isolated, but fiercely protective of you. I had intended to keep that promise.

It was a short while after you turned five that Mom had told me there were plans to move to Georgia and that when the time came, I would need to find somewhere else to go because rent was expensive and they wouldn't be able to afford a three bedroom townhome. I was twenty, nearly done with my associate's degree, but I felt like it was out of reach anyway. I decided at that moment that I needed to move back to our hometown and start fresh.

I lived out of boxes in my care for two and a half weeks, couch surfing every now and again just to stay warm.After I'd raised enough money, I told Mom that I was moving and that I wanted to come and say goodbye to you.

Leaving you was the most emotional parting. I gave you one of my softest blankets, one that you used to always steal from my room when I was away.

I also gave you all my barbie dolls from my childhood and a special stuffed animal.

I got down on your level and said to you. "I love you so much. I'm not leaving because of you. I'm leaving because I need to take care of me. You can call me any time. You will never be a bother. I want to hear about your day every single day if that's what you want to do. Please keep yourself safe. Don't let anybody do anything to you that you don't want to be done."

Then I gave you the biggest hug, and that's when I promised you that when you were older I would tell you something very important.

My dear Ayla, that time is now. I never want you to think that I abandoned you. I stayed with you as long as I could. Now that you're 15, the same age I was, I want you to know that if anything were to happen to you, if anyone hurt you or violated you, or you got in trouble and you needed someone trustworthy to lean on, it doesn't matter how far away I am. I promised I would always protect you and I intend to do just that.

All the love in the world.

Your Sister, Hera

About the Author

Heather Picardat is a Grand Rapids native, artist, writer and photographer with a passion for nature and all things poetic. Her style is mostly comprised of a direct and heartfelt exploration of hard-to-discuss topics that mirror firsthand experiences from her life. Through skillful storytelling and emotional prose, her thought-provoking journeys offer a glimpse into the complexities of real-life situations that sometimes challenge one's beliefs, emotional responses and, ultimately, their empathetic nature.

Adult Published Finalist

Gristle, Witch Hazel, and the Kickball
Maggie Roberts VanHaften

Lizzy Campbell marched down the gravel road, head held high, confidence rising from her body like heat off asphalt on a 90-degree day.

The kids would have to let her play kickball today. Afterall, cradled in her arms was her birthday present: a real, official kickball. Genuine.

Not like the beat-up rubber balls they usually used. Dickie Griswald, known as 'Gristle' because he was so mean and ornery, refused to let her play, probably because she was a better player at nine than he was at twelve.

Nevertheless, he considered himself the boss of the neighborhood kids and denied her the chance join in. None of the kids dared stand up to him. Yet, with the wisdom that comes with advanced age, Lizzy assumed the lure of playing with an official ball would get the other kids to over-rule him.

She passed Mr. Harden's driveway. Lizzy considered him the coolest person she knew; he had a brand-new car, a blue Edsel with a front grille that looked like the mouths of the Kissing Gouramis in her fishbowl. Even cooler, after Henry Oliver got hit by a car while playing baseball in the road, Mr. Harden had cleared his spare lot. The kids could play there only if they followed his rules: no fighting, no rock throwing, all play stops when the streetlight comes on, and no kicking or tossing a ball over the side fence into Miss Hazel Poppin's yard.

Hazel Poppin, widely known as 'Witch Hazel,' was a legend in the Mill Creek neighborhood. Lizzy knew two things about her. First, she kept the balls that went into her yard; no one ever dared to ask for a wayward ball to be returned. Second, it was well known to the kids in the neighborhood that she grabbed children who ventured onto her porch, hauled them into her kitchen, and cut them up as the secret ingredient in her banana-nut bread. Johnny Siegel said the kid-meat added bulk to the batter. Nancy Trevlin swore she heard that Witch Hazel used extra nutmeg to cover the taste of kid-guts in the bread. And, Eldon Schwartz believed the Old Witch ground the remaining bones and spread the powder in her garden as fertilizer, which was why her azaleas and hydrangeas were so bountiful - he'd personally witnessed her doing just that.

Gristle, however, deemed himself the authority on Witch Hazel. To date, none of the kids within the neighborhood had ever turned up missing, but Gristle knew ones who had. Martin Quinn and Angela McDonald disappeared suddenly, and while the kids' parents said the Quinn family had moved to Seattle and the McDonalds to Wichita, Gristle said he had seen Witch Hazel grab the kids from her porch when they went collecting for *UNICEF*.

Halloween presented a dilemma because if a kid trick-or-treating alone stopped at Witch Hazel's house, they were not likely to get home. It would have been easy to skip her house, except Witch Hazel gave out the best treats: honest-to-goodness real Hersey bars, not the little bite-sized ones other people gave out. They figured if they all climbed the forbidden front steps together and put the little kids in front, they could run if she grabbed the closest one. Nancy reasoned the tykes were more tender, anyway.

Besides, there were parents following them in the street; the kids doubted Witch Hazel would succumb to her culinary urges with parents around.

She even dressed in costume as a nice old lady, like a grandma, just to fool them. Once the treasured treats were in their possession, they were faced with the dilemma of whether to eat the bars or toss them away because they might contain mouse-turds or spiders. It had become routine for the kids to smash the bars and, finding no foreign matter, consume them with no ill-effects. But that was Halloween, two months away, and not part of Lizzy's thoughts. Kickball was. Lizzy wasn't concerned about it ending up in Witch Hazel's yard because she was sure the ball couldn't be kicked high enough to clear Witch Hazel's fence.

As she approached the lot, Trisha Melbourne hollered, "Hey, what've you got there?"

"A real, genuine kickball. Got it for my birthday yesterday."

"Did ja say a kickball?" It was Gristle, sneering, his chest thrust out, his buck teeth jutting over his bottom lip like he did when he was trying to be menacing.

"I'll bet it ain't real, leemee see it."

"It is too real! It says so right on the ball...better than that old rubber ball you've got."

But Lizzy held it tight as she walked towards him, unwilling to relinquish her treasure until she was assured she could join. "You can only use it if I can play."

"You're just a wimp of a kid. We'll grind your sorry excuse of a body into the dust."

"Then I'm going home," said Lizzy. She took a step to leave, trusting that the chance to play with a real kickball would be too much for the other kids.

They started shouting at Gristle to let her play. She could see his determined expression weaken.

"Don't be such a baby. You can play."

"Promise?"

"Ya, honest. Think I'd lie?" He looked out at Skip McDougal. "Hey Skippy, I said she could play, right?"

"That's what I heard."

"Just don't cry when I beat your sorry little ass. Give me the dang ball and let's get this game goin.'"

Lizzy took a step closer; she could smell his rancid odor. Gristle jerked the ball from her arms. "Now Lizard, get lost." Lizzy tried to grab the ball back, but Gristle just heaved it over to Skippy, and when she went after Skippy, he tossed it to Tonio Spenelli. By the time Lizzy got to him, he'd launched it back to Gristle. Lizzy ran to Gristle, who held it just out of her reach.

Lizzy's chest was pounding as she jumped to grab it.

"Oh, just give it to her," said Angela VanDerHaven.

But Gristle shoved the ball between his side and his left arm and thrust his right arm hard into Lizzy's back, adding a kick that sent her sprawling into the gravel. She skidded on her hands and knees, scraping them open.

She watched stunned as he launched the ball with a mighty kick, not to the fielders, but to his left, over the fence. The kids watched in disbelief as it bounced onto Witch Hazel's roof then slid off, probably landing in her prized azalea bushes.

The kids froze only a moment, then ran. Gristle yelled over his shoulder, "Now you can have your ball, Lizard," and was gone.

Tears started flowing down Lizzy's cheeks as the blood from her skinned knees streamed down her shins. What hurt worse than her knees and hands was her pride; she hung her head in agony. Trisha ran back and, grabbing her arm, dragged Lizzy's behind the Morton's Studebaker.

From there they could see Witch Hazel come out and stride to her azalea bush and then to the ball that had broken off pink flowers. She picked up the ball, looked up and down the street, causing Trisha and Lizzy to press themselves closer to car.

"Maybe she'll give it back…"

"Not worth the gamble," said Trisha with that eleven-year-old air of authority. "You know what they say." The pair peeked around once more to watch Witch Hazel take the ball into her house.

"I didn't even get to play with it," cried Lizzy as she noticed the sand and gravel ground into her knees and the blood pooling in the cuffs of her socks.

Trisha said, "Better get home. Go through Hinkleman's back yard to stay out of sight and get those knees cleaned up so you don't get gangrene or something." And she was off.

Lizzy limped through backyards to her make-shift hideout in her dad's garage. She stopped only to pick up some paper towel from his workbench.

She spit on the towel and did her best to clean her wounds. She was glad her mom was at Mrs. Lawrence's book club; she didn't want sympathy.

Lizzy wanted to hurt. And her knees and hands did hurt, but not as much as her heart. It was shattered. She was angry - really angry. She seethed. She wanted revenge.

She wanted Witch Hazel to bake Gristle into banana-nut bread and feed it to Skippy and Tonio. This thought momentarily eased the tears. But what she really wanted was her ball back.

She was tired of being the little kid, of being bullied, of not fitting in, not with the younger girls in the neighborhood and not with the bigger kids.

She fit nowhere. She was tired of being shoved around. She plotted how she could get back at Gristle; but couldn't come up with more than fantasies like smearing his bike seat with dog poop or his handlebars with poison ivy.

All sorts of vile ideas came to her. But in the end, she knew none would result in her getting her ball back.

Then, it came to her. She could get her ball back one way. It was risky and she didn't want to deliberate too much or she wouldn't do it. She'd count to four, then she'd go...1...2...3.........4. She got up and, despite her burning knees, planted her left foot on the garage floor, then her right, one after the other with determination. She pushed her shoulders back and held her head high. Ignoring her pounding heart and throbbing head, she marched down the street toward Mr. Harden's lot. The boys had returned and were playing some sort of croquet with part of an old set. They stopped when they saw her.

"Cry baby, comin' ta beat me up?" taunted Gristle, his head and chest shoved forward and a sneer on his face. But his words and expression barely registered. She just kept moving, all the way to Witch Hazel's house where she climbed the steps to the porch and knocked on the door.

Only then did she feel like bolting, but instead she held her breath. Out of the corner of her eyes she saw the boys standing at the edge of the road, jaws hanging open. In a strange way, their expressions gave her confidence: she was doing something they'd never dare to try. But those thoughts vanished as Witch Hazel appeared at the door, wiping her hands on an apron.

"Why, Elizabeth, what brings you here?"

Lizzy said nothing at first, her eyes peering around Witch Hazel to see if there were any visible caldrons or butcher knives. She couldn't see anything through the screen. Her eyes darted to Witch Hazel's face. She looked like a normal grandma.

"Elizabeth?"

Lizzy took a deep breath. "I'd like my ball back." Remembering her manners, she added, "Please." Then she trembled. "Gristle kicked it over the fence."

"Well, why don't you come in and see what we can do about that." Seeing Lizzy's hesitation, she clarified, "You know, Elizabeth, I don't cut up children and put them in my banana-nut bread; I think they'd make it sour and gritty."

Lizzy eyes moved up to Witch Hazel's face. She was smiling, not a scary smile, but a friendly one. And her eyes were twinkling. Lizzy looked at the open door, then down at her dirty, blood-stained hands; she wiped them as well as she could on her shorts. Then, she peeked again at this woman's face.

"Don't worry, we'll get you cleaned up," she said, opening the door. "I just took chocolate chips cookies out of the oven, and I need someone to taste them with me. Will you help? We can talk about your ball."

Lizzy took a deep gulp of air and entered, her eyes darting around the living room. It looked like an ordinary living room with no blood on the carpet, no chains hanging from the chairs, just a regular couch and rocker and a card table with four chairs.

"My Bridge Club is coming today. That's why I've been baking. Come on into the kitchen." Lizzy took another deep breath and followed her.

Again, her eyes darted around. The kitchen looked a lot like her mom's. No big cutting boards for chopping up kids; and the oven wasn't big enough for a kid. It was just a regular kitchen.

Witch Hazel watched Lizzy assess the kitchen; noting her eyes pausing to take in each detail. The yellow ruffled curtains matched the countertops. There was a plant on the windowsill.

And, on the kitchen table were stacks of cookies and loaves of banana-nut bread. It smelled like her grandma's kitchen. Lizzy tried to sort out what she had been told and what she was seeing.

"I think some cookies and lemonade might help those knees and hands feel better, but before that, I think we might want to wash them and put band-aids on them."

Lizzy pressed the left side of her lips together in a puzzled way. "You don't have kids, do you?"

"No, I don't."

"So how do you know how to fix skinned knees?"

"Well, I had a lot of them when I was your age, but I also was a pediatric nurse – I took care of sick and injured children."

Lizzy squished her eyebrows together imagining her as a nurse.

"Did you wear a white uniform and pointy hat?"

"I certainly did. Now, come on with me, we'll get you fixed."

And so Witch Hazel transformed into Miss Poppin before Lizzy's eyes. Nothing changed about how she looked, but something changed in Lizzy's mind.

"About this ball; it's the kickball?"

"Yes, Ma'am. I got it for my birthday yesterday and Gristle stole it from me and kicked it onto your roof and I think it rolled into your 'zaleas, and I never got to play with it." She gulped, and the tears welled up in her eyes again - maybe from the loss of the ball, maybe from the sting of the Bactine, maybe from being overwhelmed by all that was happening. Miss Poppin got another washcloth wet with cool water and smoothed it across Lizzy's dusty, tear-stained face, and then over the back of her neck. It felt like it did when Lizzy's mom did the same thing. Lizzy found that interesting, that Miss Poppin could do that.

"Now, I think we have you patched up. My prescription says you need cookies and lemonade."

Lizzy's eyes brightened. "Thank you for cleaning me up. Water works better that the spit I tried to use."

In the kitchen, each with a glass of lemonade and cookies, Miss Poppin talked about Gristle's behavior. "You know, Richard – Gristle - as you call him, doesn't have a very loving home…not a nice place to live. Mean really.

Maybe he doesn't know how else to be if that's the treatment he gets at home." Miss Poppin glanced up at Lizzy.

Lizzy pondered that; she'd never thought about why Gristle was mean. Her eyebrows wrinkled as she thought.

"We had bullies when I was your age; I got picked-on a lot. I hated them, but now I wonder about them."

Lizzy thought for a moment. "What did you do?"

"Oh, I tried to avoid them. But, if I had the answer to how to handle bullies, other that, why, I'd be President." She paused, "So why do you want to play with him?"

Lizzy thought about this for a moment, her brows once again pressed together. "I guess I want to play kickball and they're the only kids around who know how."

"It's easy for me to say find other kids, but not so easy to do. But in case you haven't noticed, Gristle and his buddies are standing by the corner of my yard, and have been since you came in. They're afraid of me; you're not.

Just remember that. Now, about that ball…"

Miss Poppin got up and went to the closet, bringing back a bag of balls. "Here's yours," she said, handing the kickball to Lizzy. Then she pulled out others, most with a name taped to it.

"I did my best to identify who they belonged to." She reached for one more. "This is Gristle's baseball, actually his older brother's. He's away in the Army. It's autographed by Mickey Mantle." She handed Lizzy the bag. "I'm giving you all of them; you can decide what to do."

She paused. "Well, my bridge club will be coming soon; I'd better finish getting ready. I'm glad you came, Lizzy. Come again. I promise I won't eat you." She smiled that kind of secret smile reserved for private friends.

As they walked to the door, Lizzy had one more question. "Why'd you keep the balls?"

"No one ever came to ask for them back." Lizzy, pursed her lips, nodding thoughtfully.

Out on the street, the crowd of kids had grown, all calling out questions and asking how she avoided being baked into banana-nut bread.

"She's not a witch, just a nice lady. I had cookies and lemonade, and she gave me the balls and some banana-nut bread for my mom." With that, Lizzy started distributing the balls to as many rightful owners as she could while they crowded around her, asking a flurry of questions. Only Gristle hung back, digging his toe in the dirt, refusing to participate. Over the

next week, other kids came to get their balls from her. One was left: Gristle's autographed baseball. He never came to ask for it and never showed up for kickball games again. He faded into an unpleasant, but distant memory.

***

It's been sixty-five years since that summer. I never saw Gristle again. I regret I hadn't taken his ball to him. Maybe he'd needed a friend, but I hadn't offered. Today it sits on my bookshelf next to my very worn kickball.

About the Author

Maggie Roberts VanHaften has loved writing stories since she first picked up one of those big black "learn to print" pencils in kindergarten. Over the years, required writing for school, college, grad school and work shifted her attention from fiction to research papers, technical writing and legal filings. Finally, retirement has given her the time to return to her childhood passion, supported by her dear husband, faithful writing colleagues, and trusted family and friends. She hopes her stories connect with a few readers.

Teen Judges' Choice Winner

A House with a Garden
Sonja de Wilde

Please note that any grammatical and/or punctuational "errors" are a conscious stylistic choice made by the author to reflect both the characters and the setting of the story.

July has faded soft into the sticky August heat when the nights are no cooler than noon and I wear his old t-shirt over my underwear to bed. The silence in the trailer at the bottom of the hill has a dead kind of feeling and one of his knees is pressed into the damp back of mine as we lay on top of the covers, too hot to touch. The clock ticks on through the early morning hours and I breathe the smell of cigarettes in from the pillows. It used to make me cough when I was young but I haven't been bothered for a long time now. Everything in this town smells of smoke, steeps in it, either from the gold mine or from the broken old people holding Marlboros or Newports between trembling bent fingers on the street corners and in the motels and at the campground and in the diner on Grace Street.

It is 1:24 AM when he tells me he's been waiting for his uncle to die.

It's not because I hate him, you know, he says, voice thick in the night air.

I hope it happens real fast, like a heart attack on his way home from the prison some night. It's just because that house in my Grandpa's will was meant for me. He is quiet for a moment, I meant it for you too, you know.

I know. We've already picked the furniture and the color green that we'll paint the walls when we can call that house in the country ours. Playing our game, I ask him again, Can I have a garden?

He says again that it had better be thirty feet tall.

I know why he wants that house so badly. Growing up parked in the campground for so long took away any softness he had left in him as a boy.

His calloused fingers trace circles on my arms in the wet southern heat and the heaviness of his hand is not lost on me. But I've seen him feed the stray dogs made of bones and the outline of his broken nose when he smokes out the window at sunrise before his shift and I know that somewhere inside him is a boy who misses his father and grandfather and what he could have been.

In the morning the windows are cracked to let the stirrings of a breeze through, and a fresh ring of bruises blooms around my wrist where he held onto the world through his nightmares. The old ones stain green and yellow under deep purple. I have never minded the colors, or being a tether.

Strange things walk the night here. I dress in a pair of his cutoff denim shorts (I've hardly worn my own clothes since he was forced into working at the mine and I've gotten used to the feeling of the waist hanging low on the bones of my hips), straighten the sheets, and pour a glass of water from the tap. The no-name dogs wait at the back door where a scuffed metal bowl sits at the bottom of the steps and I pour the glass in and the mutts lap wildly for a mouthful, not minding that the water is lukewarm. I set the glass back in the sink and get my sandals from the mat by the front door, locking it behind me.

The town is quiet this early. Well, it's always quiet, but in the mornings it might as well be a ghost town. Most of the men have already gone to work like mine, and the women are inside, taking advantage of the only slightly cooler dawn to clean and cook. The diner on Grace Street only holds a few of the elderly, their faces deeply lined and their eyes sunken. I get a cheese sandwich for breakfast and some eggs, hard-boiled. The few cents left over go into Old John's beggar's cup on the way to the store. The hard-boiled eggs I split in half and feed to the toothless dogs in the weedy park one by one. They thump their spiny tails against the overgrowth and lick my fingers with their cracked tongues and warm gums.

At the grocery store I buy the last box of sweet breakfast cereal, a piece of red meat - some kind of steak - and a few softened vegetables, just past ripe. The woman behind the counter, Mary Lou (the kind of person who has nothing better to do than theorize and gossip), gives me a once over.

Those clothes are a little big, don't you think, dear? she says, her painted mouth wide in a smile, voice dripping chemical sweetness. It will not be the last time she makes this remark.

They aren't mine, is all I say back to her as I dig out a crumpled twenty dollar bill from the back pocket of his shorts.

She frowns as she hands me the receipt, *Hon, you're both too young to be living this kind of life... Not even twenty-one, neither of you-* I walk away before I hear the rest.

The night has set in deep and dark when he finally unlocks the front door and steps in, worn and tired. I unlace his work boots and unbutton the heavy overshirt covered in grime. I lead him to the bathroom, where the tub sits full under the yellow lights, and undo his belt and jeans before helping him sink into the water.

We both watch as it slowly turns black.

I cover my hands in soap and work it into his hair before moving to knead out the knots in his shoulders. When I dig my thumbs in, he hisses curse words through his teeth, and all I can think about is how when that house out in the country is the place we'll call home, the ache will stop. I tell him that over and over from where I sit on the edge of the bathtub, that the ache will stop.

The meat is seasoned well and we eat in silence, listening to the dogs bark outside and the crackle of a bonfire somewhere out in the campground surrounded by loud voices. Those are the real campers, the people who come here for the mountains and the forest and can leave when they grow weary. I wash the dishes and turn the lights off before joining him in bed.

Tonight is less muggy than it's been in weeks and he curls around me and I feel the heat of him on my back and my legs and the smell of our soap drowns out the smoke and I love him, I love him, I love him.

I wake up sometime just before 3 AM. Something feels strange and the shadows are too dark and for the first time in my eighteen years I am freezing in my tank top and shorts. I roll over, away from the red light of the clock and towards him, but when I reach out all I feel are tangled sheets.

It's only then that I sit up and really open my eyes. The bedroom door is open and the short hallway to the rest of the trailer is dark, but I can see the moon coming in through one of the windows in the kitchen. We never leave the door open.

I whisper his name into the dark, a question with no answer.

There is no sign of him as I walk through the trailer, but the back door is open, hanging by one bolt and creaking in the breeze. When I reach it, the five dark rips in the metal become clearer and I've never seen a bobcat or a coyote or even the black bears that we sometimes get around here leave marks that big. I fit my own fingers into the slashes and they sink a half inch into the door, which sways awkwardly on its single hinge.

Our trailer backs up to the woods at the bottom of the hill and when I turn to glance outside, the trees are still and quiet. I flip on the outside light, which only reaches about five feet from the back door, but it's enough for me to walk down the steps and really look. I call his name, not a whisper but soft enough that I won't bother anyone in the campground. The returning silence is overwhelming. I move to the very edge of the half circle of light, treading hesitantly in the dewy grass, and call again. Nothing. My stomach sinks further and after a moment I take a few steps into the dark and closer to the tree-line.

Something moves behind the branches and I freeze. A shining pair of eyes reflects the trailer's light back at me. I see it stiffen and shift forward and I stumble back as it slowly lopes closer to the edge of the woods. When it nears the tree-line it straightens up to walk on its two hind legs. It clears seven feet easily and as it steps out into the clearer space I see the horrible entirety of it.

Its head is shaped a little like a coyote, with a pointed snout and ears, but it has far too many teeth, all bared. A pair of smoky black antlers burst from the top of its head between its ears, which are set lower than a canine's. The full eight point rack shifts and curls like it's not entirely solid. The creature stands on its back legs, which are digitigrade like a wolf's, and its arms hang at its sides, long-fingered paws tipped with claws made of the same dark mist as the antlers.

It is blacker than the dirt of the gold mine, except for its teeth and eyes, which glimmer strangely like the veins that run through the dark rock.

There is a moment when I meet its gaze, its slit pupils locked on mine.

A chill runs through me down to my bones, like it has shaken my soul, and I feel goosebumps rise on my skin in the warm air. I look away fast, still backing towards the trailer. It lowers itself to all fours as I near the light and a low growl escapes its throat, a sound that I know even now I will never forget. As soon as it moves forwards, my instincts take over and I am running for the trailer as fast as I can, breaking every rule of dealing with a hunting animal; but this isn't a normal predator. When I reach the trailer I pull the broken door closed as hard as I can, but it opens outwards and I know I can't hold it on its single hinge. I feel the whole trailer shake when the creature hits it with a roar that sounds more human than animal and I lurch away, looking for a hammer, a tool, *anything*.

I come up with the butcher's knife I used to cut the meat for dinner, still sitting in the sink. It won't be enough, I can tell.

The door is ripped completely off the hinges and the creature shoves its way in, snarling and huge and pitch-black. I whirl to face it and grip the knife tighter, backed into the kitchen. It stalks closer, antlers drawing lines in the ceiling plaster, filling the trailer like a void. Fear and adrenaline beat through me in equal parts, and I raise the knife as it bares its teeth, its jaws only about four feet from where my back has hit the kitchen wall, the lightswitch digging into my skin through the fabric of my shirt. I've dealt with animals before, but this *thing* is more terrifying than anything I have ever seen, and a feeling seeps off of it, panic and desperation. My eyes fill with tears because I don't want to die, I don't want to die here alone, I don't want to die without him. I see it lunge in slow motion, mouth open.

I scream, louder than I ever have, and I can feel it rip out from somewhere deep in my throat as the tears spill over down my cheeks and the knife connects with something solid. The creature snarls in pain and I let go of the handle as it pulls its hand away, the knife stuck clean through the middle, black blood dripping from the wound. It shakes its arm, ripping out the knife, which clatters back against the kitchen counter. I can't help it, I sink down to the floor against the wall, shaking and unable to stop my tears as the creature looms in a crouch over me, its breath hot and smelling of decay. Its claws rake down into my arms and I let out a cry of pain and turn my face away so I won't see it rip its teeth into me.

But it never does.

Slowly I turn my head to look back at it, and find it frozen just inches from my face. The pupils of its eyes shift in the green iris. One moment they are near invisible vertical slits, and the next they're wide circles before flickering to ovals and then back again. It backs away, bumping into the table and knocking a bowl to the ground where it shatters. Its hands clutch at its head, and it shrieks, another sound I will never forget. Its howl is more anguished than mine as it folds into itself and the vapory darkness of the antlers and claws swirl and dissipate, its ears shortening, limbs cracking into place until all that is left is...

Him, curled on his side and shivering on the moonlit floor in his nightclothes, one of his hands in his hair, the other pulled close to his chest, bleeding from a gash in the palm and through to the back just below his knuckles. A black mist is already knitting it back together. I gasp for air through sobs, adrenaline fading into shock, but I can't move from where I sit pressed against the wall, unable to slow my breathing. I hardly even notice the sticky warmth tracing down my arms.

It's only when I see that he's crying that I finally unfreeze. I crawl across the floor, the ceramic pieces of the broken bowl digging into my hands and knees, and I reach out to touch him before I realize that the long-healed scars on his back from his step-father's belt are open again, bleeding a little more with every heave of his ribcage. I get to my feet, still breathing uneven, and stumble to the sink where I fumble for a dish towel and soak it under the lukewarm tap. It doesn't occur to me to turn the water off before I kneel beside him again. His ribbed undershirt is ripped apart and I pull the rest off so I can press the cloth to his back. His body jerks when I touch him and I flinch away fast.

I'm sorry- his voice is broken through tears. I'm sorry, I'm sorry-

I move to face him and help him sit up, on my knees in front of him. He wraps his arms around me like a lifeline and presses his face into my torso.

I run my hands through his hair and pick the towel off the floor to flatten against the slashes in his back. I let him cry into me and I remind him of our dream, just like I do every time he gets angry or tired or beaten down by this town and everything it means to him.

We'll have a soft life in that house out in the country and we'll walk out into the garden in the early morning, a garden so tall we can't see over it.

We'll paint the walls green and buy the furniture from the catalog in the kitchen drawer.

We will be happy.

Somebody knocks on the front door of the trailer, asks if we're alright. I tell her everything's fine, just a little fight. Everybody fights here. They've been fighting for years before the gold mine opened, and they'll be fighting long after it closes down, worn to nothing but rock.

We will never get out of this trailer and the house will go to his uncle's new wife and daughter. The creature will come back, often and unpredictably. I will take care of him until the gold dust in his lungs and the darkness in his body catch up and take him from me too early. The old miners in their coveralls who called him June, short for Junior and for the month he was born in, will stand with me at the funeral. His family will not attend.

I will grow older missing half of myself, reminded of him in everything.

I will feed the stray dogs every morning and never fix the back door. I will die here in these hills.

About the Author

Sonja de Wilde is a high school junior who has been writing all her life. While she hopes to be a marine biologist and an auto mechanic, she knows she'll always be writing both music and stories on the side. Guitar is her favorite instrument, and she's working on getting her scuba diving certification. Inspired by the gothic South and stories of love and loss, "A House With A Garden" follows the third act of her concept album of the same name (unpublished). She dedicates her story to Sofia.

Teen Judges' Choice Runner-Up

Mist Men
Finn Rice

From his satchel, he removed and unrolled a crimson red piece of silk - it was square and about the size of his hand. Golden lace adorned the edges. He gently placed it down upon the cold mossy rock of the well's edge. Its bright red sheen glowed against the dull gray stone. He reached back into his satchel and retrieved a teapot; golden and spotless. The pot was unusually small - probably too small to practically serve tea to even one person. Slowly and gently, he placed the pot upon the silk. As he set it down, its golden exterior seemed to grow brighter. He reached back into his satchel for a third time, and retrieved a small but seemingly sharp knife.

With his left hand, he held the knife above the open tea pot. With his right, he pressed his thumb to the knife's edge. The moment flesh made contact with steel, a small gash formed and scarlett droplets fell into the pot. The pot seemed to grow even brighter. As he held his thumb above it, the man did not wince or show any signs of pain. It seemed almost as if he had done this before. After several moments, he returned the knife to his satchel and stood up. The wound in his thumb was already closing up. In a few seconds, it would be impossible to tell that the skin had ever been breached.

Now, he peered over the well's edge. Within its circle of stone, it contained a black abyss with no indication of depth. Only darkness stretching on for as far as one could imagine. The man looked back at the teapot. He took it by the handle, held it above the well, and began to pour.

Out came a stream of his blood. The scarlet liquid traveled down the well and into the darkness. The teapot only took a few moments to empty itself. The man then returned it to his satchel, and sat down cross-legged on the soft moss in front of the well. He lowered his head and closed his eyes.

***

Several hours had gone by. The once bright sun was beginning to lower itself below the horizon, and it was casting a warm orange glow upon the greenery and the man resting in it. The glow slowly stretched across his face, like a hand reaching to gently wake him. Still sitting cross-legged, he raised his head before standing up. He leaned over and peered into the well. As he did so, a sound came echoing out of it. It was the gentle splash of his own blood reaching the well's unseen floor. Next, a red mist began rising out of the well - it sparkled as if it contained the stars of a thousand universes. The mist began moving and forming shapes. First, it created the impression of two broad eyebrows. Then, the outline of a sharp nose and a firm mouth. Lastly, two sparkling stars in the mist grew to create shining eyes. Fully formed, the mist-man wore an expression of tired resolve. He turned to face the satchel-bearing man responsible for his summoning.

The mist parted where his mouth was.

"I remember you." He spoke with a perpetual sigh. "Atticus." As he enunciated every syllable, his star-filled eyes would brighten and then dim, brighten and then dim. The satchel-bearing man named Atticus stood before the mist-man with slumped shoulders. One might have assumed from his conserved silhouette that Atticus was afraid, but his weary eyes and aged face indicated that he was really just tired. Not the kind of tiredness that vanished with a night's rest, but the kind that accumulated over years and never let go - like the chilling grasp of death, ever tightening. Everything about his appearance indicated this. His hair was dull and white - barely clinging to his head. Wrinkles painted his face and invisible weights seemed to pull down his skin.

Atticus raised his head to stare into the eyes of the mist.

"I want you to undo it." He spoke in creaks and groans - whatever his voice had once sounded like, it was now eroded by age.

The mist spoke back.

"I said I remembered you. I didn't say I remembered what I did for you. Start from the beginning." The mist-man seemed tired yet commanding.

"I was a lad when I found you. Asked for immortality. Said I wanted to live forever."

"Oh yes. That was amusing."

"You granted my wish. Didn't warn me or nothing. Sent me on my way, like pushing a child off a cliff."

"I'm only a humble servant. Just here to bend and contort myself to the wishes of humans. Then screw off when they're done using me." His words could have been interpreted as sarcasm, but the complete lack of a shift in tone made it impossible to tell. Atticus seemed as though he had nearly mustered a chuckle, but all that escaped was a wheeze.

"Suppose immortality wasn't what I thought it was."

"The thought never occurred to you that living forever would mean witnessing every tragedy to come and never being able to form meaningful relationships again?"

"Try telling that to someone when they've got the option right in front of them."

"That doesn't make it my problem. Why should I concern myself with the lives of humans?" As he spoke, the mist-man's semi-transparent head grew brighter. "I have existed for millennia before humans. I have served a basic function so that I might remain unbothered. When the Earth is swallowed by the Sun and every organism on this planet is ground down to an intangible dust, I will still exist, somewhere, always present." The mist-man kept growing brighter until everything around him was bathed in a harsh red glow. His once tired voice was growing in volume, though his tone was still unchanging. He seemed to worm his way into Atticus' ears, pressuring his eardrums until they seemed as though they might explode.

Atticus fell to his bony knees, closing his eyes and putting his hands over his ears. The mist-man was no longer speaking, but his mouth was open and a deep roar was perpetually escaping it. Atticus could feel his ears pooling with blood. The sound was vibrating his eardrums so violently that they seemed to be disintegrating. Yet for every miniscule piece of muscle that was torn apart by sound, another would grow in its place. Atticus yelled with all of the shrill force his eternally aging throat could muster.

"Wait! Stop!"

The booming ceased. In an instant, the violent red light retreated and the surrounding forest returned itself to hues of green awash in sunset. Atticus slowly rose to his feet. His posture was still conserved, but it wasn't just age that weighed him down now - it was fear. The immortal man found himself afraid of something. It was a feeling he had almost forgotten. Death was never a concern to him, but the constant pain the mist-man had subjected him to seemed worse.

He remembered why he had come here: so that he could die. The mist-man, still wearing a face of indifference, despite his obvious anger, spoke:

"You aren't the first who has wanted me to undo your own mistakes.

All I do is give you what you ask, and still you are not satisfied. Have you changed your mind? Will you leave?"

"Can't you just do it?", said Atticus. There was desperation in his voice.

"You gave it to me in an instant. Surely..." . His voice trailed off. The mist-man was beginning to lower into the well. His eyes were closed and the stars within him were fading. Atticus rushed towards the well, his age evident as he moved like a rusted piece of machinery. He rapidly grasped at the mist. His hands passed through it, yet he continued to try to grab the mist-man, a look of both horror and desperation on his face.

"No, no!", he screamed. "I can't go on! It's torture!". No response. The red head full of stars disappeared into the darkness of the well. Atticus leaned over the edge of the well. He stood still for only a second, and then jumped in.

***

He had fallen for an unknowable amount of time. For a while, he was able to look up and see the light above the well, but the light had grown smaller as he fell, and eventually disappeared. Atticus was falling into pitch-black nothingness, unsure when his journey would end. He wasn't exactly alone with his thoughts as he fell - the adrenaline had overridden his brain and all he could think about was the moment when he smacked against the deep dark well bottom and broke most of his bones. Sometimes he would run his hand along the cold brick interior of the well and remind himself he was in a tangible place and not an endless abyss.

Suddenly there came a moment when the bricks of the well seemed to disappear. Atticus stretched his arms out, but couldn't feel the claustrophobic walls he had almost grown used to. Maybe he was in an abyss now. Sometime while he was falling, he contemplated his future.

Maybe he would become some kind of twisted Prometheus, falling forever, blinded in the dark - eternal torture. Or maybe there was a bottom. The mist-man probably dwelled down there. Undoubtedly he would want to hurt Atticus, punish him for his supposed arrogance... like some kind of twisted Prometheus. He only saw pain in his future.

***

There was a bottom. When he hit it, the smack would have been deafening, if there was anyone to hear it. His blood exploded across the ground, as did much of his flesh and bone. Atticus went momentarily unconscious, before awakening to nothing but pain. Being immortal, he had developed a tolerance to lethal injuries, but this hurt like nothing he had ever known. As he lay there, he tried to find solace in the fact that he was immortal and that the pain would go away and he would be returned to normal. His body was slowly mending itself, removing the pain. First bone grew out of itself, in the shape of a human skeleton. Then muscle seemed to grow out of bone. It wrapped itself around the bone like a coat. Organs formed beneath it all and resumed their bodily functions. Finally, skin grew out of muscle, appearing old and withered despite its sudden creation.

Whole again, Atticus stayed lying on the ground. He found himself facing the sudden fear of going on, and potentially facing greater pain. He wished in that moment that he could find peace in his immortality. That he could do something that would satisfy him for eternity. He knew it was pointless. Just like he had chosen to be immortal in a moment when his greed blinded him, he had jumped down this well when his desperation blinded him. His life was dictated by his deepest flaws. He had only ever become tangled in his desires.

First he regretted immortality, then he regretted chasing the cure. If he stood up and went on, Atticus felt he would only dig himself deeper. Instead he lay down and thought about his life. He had been to every place anyone would want to see in the world. If he wanted to learn a language, he had the time to do it. He had picked up most skills a person could reasonably want. He played by the rules of the world and became infinitely successful.

That was all within 100 years. Atticus had been alive for 2,000. He had convinced himself immortality was everything he could want. After living for so long, he knew that dream was only an illusion he created to make it bearable. Yet still, he was afraid to lose it all and die like everyone else. So he never returned to the mist-man. Not until he met someone, and decided he wanted to die with them, rather than outlive yet another soul. When he realized he loved them, he had suddenly felt the immense weight of his selfishness upon his back. It was the influence of another that finally conquered his fear of death, if only to replace it with a fear of loss. Now here he was, confined to a place of horrors unknown while someone waited for him on the outside. Atticus' immense fear of the abyss he found himself in seemed to war with his desire to return to the one he loved.

Atticus was frozen in conflict, unable to move. He lay there for longer than he had been falling in the well, waiting for something - maybe the mist-man - to come looking for him. He knew pain would follow, but it was an easier fate to reckon with than having to take action against unknown forces of darkness and likely fail.

Since Atticus' body had finished healing, he began to pay attention to his surroundings. He had felt something wet surrounding him when he landed, but he hadn't paid attention to it given the overwhelming pain.

Still unable to make himself stand up, he lay down until he realized he was in some sort of liquid.

The pitch-black of the abyss prevented him from recognizing it with sight, but the metallic scent in the air told him it was blood. He reckoned it was a pool of blood from all of the humans who offered sacrifice for a chance at fantastical power. The pool was quite shallow, as Atticus was only partially submerged while laying down. However, when only a drop of blood was needed, this could represent the wishes of thousands. Atticus thought about that and wondered what the use of the blood was. He had never considered that when performing the ritual - the particulars don't really seem to matter when immortality is on the table.

Atticus tilted his head to the side and drank some of the blood. He didn't know what compelled him to do it. Maybe it was the idea of putting a part of all these people inside himself. They had all willingly given something to this pool, and now he was taking it, and becoming a vessel for their hopes and dreams of power. Or was it a way to spite the mist-man? Atticus figured the blood served some purpose to him, be it practical or symbolic.

He kept drinking, stopping only to gasp for breath. He turned over and fully submerged his face in the blood, taking in as much as he could with each gulp. Some sort of anger possessed him as he drank. Anger at the mist-man for giving him power without warning, anger at all of the people who gave their blood and got power, who were living lives without the deep pain Atticus now knew. Anger at his lover, purely for existing and pushing him to return to the well. Atticus kept drinking until his lungs hurt from taking in nothing but harsh breaths. He didn't stop until there was nothing left in the pool but a layer of blood too shallow for him to drink. He turned back over and collapsed on his back, breathing heavily.

As he lay there, too exhausted to reason with what he had done, his body began to glow. He was emitting a harsh red light - Atticus recognized it as the same as the mist-man. The light grew stronger, and then he began to dissolve.

First his feet faded away and Atticus let loose a shriek. He crawled backwards, as if to escape the light. He backed himself up against a wall of the pool, but the fading continued. It made its way up his legs, then his stomach. What remained of Atticus lay there in horror. He knew physical pain was of no threat, but this was an inconceivable force, and there was no reason to believe it couldn't destroy him permanently.

Eventually the immortal man was nothing but a head. Despite his loss of vital organs, he was still completely conscious. The dissolving had seemed to stop, but Atticus' head was still glowing red. The glow grew stronger, and his head began to change. It was not dissolving, but transforming into a mist. All of his facial features stayed, but they were not formed by bone, muscle, and skin.

His head was made of red mist, and it sparkled the same as the mist-man.

The head began to rise and grow in size, until it was floating above the pool, the same size as the mist-man.

Atticus smiled as all of the terror seemed to escape him. He understood what had happened. One power had been exchanged for a stronger one.

His immortality had led to boredom and fear. Now he had new powers, new ways to make the world his plaything. He willed himself to move, and he began to rise up through the abyss and into the well. With just a slight increase in concentration, his speed exponentially rose. The interior stone of the well became a blur, and seconds later, he was back above ground. Out of the abyss, he may have felt relief, if his mind was not already intoxicated with power. At that moment, he did not consider what this power meant.

He did not stop to think of the consequences. He only reveled in it, like he had in his immortality.

Atticus thought of going to his lover, and giving them immortality. Then he would no longer have anything to fear. Unlimited power and someone to share it with. Surely this could only be a good thing.

About the Author

Finn Rice was born in Kentucky and moved to Michigan in 2019. He is currently a senior at International Academy West in White Lake and will be attending The College of Wooster in Ohio in the fall of 2024. He plans to major in English. He has been passionate about reading and writing since a young age.

Teen Readers' Choice Winner

Omaha and Fire

Eli Ferguson

I shakily climbed off of our transport ship and onto a net ladder. It was loose and made out of rope, shaking with the wind and the sway of Normandy's turbulent waters. We were loading onto something called a "Higgins Boat".

It looked weird, almost completely like a rectangle. The bottom was completely flat and it had a man-sized ramp on the front that would drop upon hitting the beach. It scared me to look at it. It was no hardship to figure out that as soon as the ramp dropped, a rain of fire would tear through the boat and kill half the men inside. And then, as I dropped down into the boat, I thanked god that I ended up in the back, shielded by a collection of at least thirty other people. I knew it was a selfish thought, but I allowed myself to be relieved by it anyway.

And then, at once, we were off. Us and the tens, maybe hundreds of other landing craft. For a while at least, it wasn't as climactic as expected. So I started thinking, and praying, and hoping. Thinking about where I was supposed to be, which was definitely not here. I was supposed to be in the Pacific, fighting with my brother, Mark, in the 32nd Red Arrows. But some tired organizer must've put my name wrong, because somehow I ended up in Normandy. In Normandy with the 29th Blue and Grays, with the Marylanders and the Virginians and the Carolinians or whatever they are called. And I got angry.

Do I sound like a Virginian?! I thought, Does my voice sound Southern?! No! I sound like a Michigander! I sound like a Midwesterner!

"What are you so mad about, kid? You look like a tomato," said some random soldier next to me. His voice was gruff and Southern.

I looked at him. His face was the kind of face you look at and immediately think looks wise, with a red beard and greasy hair. To be honest, he looked like a lumberjack in a soldier's clothing.

"Nothing," I responded. He looked at me funny and then looked back forward. And then I continued thinking.

I had nothing to survive for. No wife, no kids, and probably no brother by the war's end. This too, was selfish thinking. But when you are about to die, you don't think of much else besides pessimistic thoughts. Either way, I berated myself in my head.

Don't think such selfish things! I told myself, What if he does survive and you don't? You ungrateful-BOOM!

An eruption of sounds and colors flew around us all at once as a boat next to us went up in flames, bullets suddenly flying in every direction and pinging off the sides of our ship. Even though we weren't in any danger, and I knew it, I ducked, afraid of even the sound of gunfire. My ears rang from the explosion and I gripped my rifle tight.

Another explosion went off in the water only feet away from us, sending a piece of shrapnel straight through the left wall and into a man's shoulder.

He screamed shortly and fell down, forcing others to cramp. I panicked and kneed down to look for any way to stop the copious amounts of blood coming from his arm, but there was no time and the gate opened and bullets ripped through and people fell down and I just made myself flat in fear. I sat like that for a minute or two and watched soldiers fall, pull themselves up and over the side of the boat, or run out the front against all odds. I could feel warm blood ooze onto me from the bodies around me, and I nearly puked. But nothing came out. I just cried, and when the bullets shifted elsewhere, I got up and ran.

After what seemed like an eternity of endless running, I tripped and face-planted into a crater. Achey, I pushed myself to come to a crouch. There were two other men. One I did not know at all, and the other was the man with a gruff voice. They sat, facing me, not saying a word. Neither of them looked as bad as me, but they were certainly just as traumatized, eyes wide open as if a ghost had just passed by. The man with the gruff voice pulled me by my collar to the side of the crater which was closest to the enemy.

"Are you crazy, standing there like that?! You'll surely get killed by a sniper.

I am surprised that you weren't butchered by one of Hitler's Buzzsaws on the way up here... Though you look like you were." He stared at me for a moment before continuing, "What happened? I see heaps of blood on you, but you yourself aren't bleeding any." He spoke with authority, so I assumed he was a Sergeant.

"Sir, I got caught in the boat for a few minutes, sir." I spoke in an exhausted tone. He relaxed and realized he was still holding my collar, so he let go. I read his name tag, which read Sergeant Brennan. I opened my mouth to speak, but another explosion went off in the sand next to us, and we all instinctively flinched. A helmet rolled into the crater, charred and with a broken strap.

I finally let myself puke.

As we sat there, waiting for an opportunity t0 present itself, a tank rolled over a crater next to us. The Sergeant's eyes widened, and realizing that this would most likely be our only chance to move, he motioned us all to get behind the tank. He jumped up first, bolting to the cover of the Sherman, followed by me. We moved slowly and hunched with the tank, watching as the third man sat in fear. As we got farther and farther away he seemed to make a decision, hopping out of the crater. I guess a sniper had seen us running and trained himself on us, because as soon as his head peeked out of protection, a spark went off on his helmet and he dropped to the floor with wide eyes. From our angle we couldn't see what he looked like after he fell, but most certainly he was dead. There wasn't anything we could do but continue walking with the cover of the tank, and as we did so more joined in a small convoy. I looked out over the beach and saw others struggling: volleys of fire kicking dirt around a man before he violently fell to the ground, people erupting into dust as artillery hit them, and even a man just standing there like he was finished with it all, staring at the bunkers we tried to protect ourselves from. I looked away right as he was shot. Eventually, I decided to look at the ground. I felt that my sickness was only growing stronger as my stomach turned with the sight of each dying soldier, the water stained red like a salty wine and the air thick with smoke.

By the time we were within twenty yards of the trenches, we became a target.

Men in the trenches located on the beach and machine gunners up the grass hill started firing rounds at us, taking out two men immediately and throwing them to the ground. Before anybody could disperse, the tank erupted into flames and sparks, throwing me backwards into the sand. My helmet strap gave away as I fell, so I had no protection for my head as I smashed to the ground, turning the world into a dizzy mess.

I could not hear, as my ears were ringing too loud, and I could not see, as my headache engulfed my vision with pain. I looked around me, attempting to make out a safe place to hide, and saw a small crater on my right. Though I tried to get up, my arms and legs wouldn't move, tired. I could not convince my body to move, or to think, or even to breathe for a short time. All I could do was watch as other, more able men fell down under a hailstorm of bullets and kicked up sand, only two men actually making it out of the death and into the crater. One looked over at me, and back at the trenches, and then back at me again, daringly reaching out and yanking me into cover. His move would end horribly, though, as another volley of machine gun fire suppressed our position, tearing through the ground and collapsing him and...

And then darkness.

I awoke to the continued sounds of burning and gunshots just as before.

I must have only been unconscious for a moment, because the remaining man from before was still in the crater, too scared to move and eyes wide open.

I shifted my gaze to my attempted rescuer, expecting an experienced lumberjack face and red hair.

Thank god it's not him, I thought. Despite the combat, I quickly realized that this was another selfish thought and scolded myself. Again. And then my brain finally realized what it should be doing right now, and I returned to a sense of panic as if I didn't just look at a body and take a moment to think good thoughts because it wasn't my friend that died during a battle.

And while I wanted to stay right there, safe from the gunfire, it seemed my instincts kicked in because I automatically used what little strength I had left to get on my knees and hands to jump into the crater. Another explosion went off around us and gunfire started spraying our position, pinning us there. I hoped to god my brother had it better off, wherever he was. Many pieces of his letter to my family had been quite literally been cut out, and all we made out was that he was somewhere in New Guinea, which wasn't much but at least we knew he was alive.

I foolishly looked over the crater and at the enemy lines, where just tens of yards away I saw packs of soldiers pressed against a wall of sand with barbed wire on the top, right out of the angle of German guns. The soldier who was next to me looked at me and said,"You aren't seriously thinking about going up, are you!?" Another bomb went off.

I gave him a nod. "You're a fool for doing this," he warned in a harsh tone.

I didn't even say a word. I just ran and ran and ran over bumps and bodies and expected to be shot like everyone else in this hellscape.

But I made it.

I nearly dove into cover at the final stretch, then getting up and sitting with my back to the sand. I looked back at the crater I came from, hoping for the other man to make the decision to run like I did. Out of the hell.

But instead I saw only an explosion, not quite on the crater but not quite on the destroyed tank. It was sort of in the middle of the two, but either way I knew that the man from before was dead.

I stared blankly for a moment, until a loud shout traveled across the thin line of soldiers who made it out of the hell.

"BANGALORES! GET BACK!"

Explosions punched holes in the barbed wire sitting atop the wall of sand intermittently, and immediately soldiers started streaming through them. I was not told to go, too, but I knew I had to. So I ran through one of them, and up the hill behind it until I was at a large stretch of trenches and bunkers at the peak of the hill, and I jumped in a little U-shaped piece that jutted out in-between two bunkers. As I jumped in, I was attacked by a German soldier with a bayonet, and without a rifle I was forced to grab and push the barrel of his rifle out of the way. The soldier, well expecting this, responded with a kick to my stomach, sending me to the ground in shock. He raised his rifle at me, thinking for a moment, ready to stab me but not quite wanting to. We looked into each other's eyes for a moment in disbelief.

He had stubble and looked no older than 17 with an oversized helmet and green eyes. He had brown hair and a very sharp jawline, with pale skin marked by a single cut from a knife, which was shallow yet still very bloody.

He relaxed a little, obviously not wanting to kill me, and I tried to stand up.

But once I was on my knees, I heard a loud POP! and the soldier fell to the floor, eyes suddenly cold and his helmet now dented. I lunged backwards. The shooter vaulted in. It was Brennan.

"You okay? I thought youd've died back at the tank," he said softly.

I didn't respond. I knew Brennan couldn't have known what had just occurred, but a man who didn't deserve it had just died. A man that otherwise would've let me survive.

"He- he was-" I attempted to say, shaken.

"It's okay. Just pick up his gun and get moving."

I reached and picked up the German weapon, and fiddled for a moment. It most obviously didn't use the same ammunition as a M1 Garand, so I looted the German of his ammunition and shamefully reloaded my new weapon.

"Alright, come on," Brennan said.

I followed him as we turned a corner slowly, but the area was clear. We continued and peeked to the right, and a sudden burst of SMG fire rang through the wood, forcing us back. I immediately reached for a grenade, hardly being able to remove the pin because of my shaky hands. I threw it as soon as the pin was out, and in just five seconds a cloud of smoke and shrapnel murdered the enemy side. We peeked again, this time without any resistance. So we continued, until finally we were right at the entrance of a bunker.

Brennan went in first, throwing in another grenade to confuse the people inside, and we rushed in as fast as we could, navigating through a miniature maze of concrete walls. On the other side were three soldiers, and Brennan shot one without hesitation before moving further up. I raised my weapon and fired as well, striking what looked to be an ammo bearer, leaving one soldier remaining. He charged with a bayonet at Brennan, so I quickly cocked my gun, but it jammed. I realized I had to reach Brennan first, so I charged with my own rifle and slammed the tip of the knife into the German's lung, sending them down and into a wall. He dropped his own gun, making a noise that resembled choking before passing out onto the floor. I didn't even have any time to think before two more Americans entered the bunker and told us to head to the rendezvous, so me and Brennan walked - surrounded by flames and the moans of the wounded - to a small, unfinished headquarters.

A man with a commanding uniform stepped out from one of the tents, holding a list and a pencil.

"Private Evans? Where is Private Evans?" His thundering yet somehow soft voice called, and I slowly walked over to him.

"Right here, sir." I felt confused. I hadn't done anything but fight, and I didn't think I was exceptional enough to get an award. Not this fast, at least.

But the reason was much, much worse than a court martial. My brother had died in New Guinea and they were sending me home so that my parents wouldn't be left without a child. I never saw Brennan again, either, but I heard he made it out alive just as well.

I fought through all of that horror and killed so many people with families of their own just for my brother to die and for me to be sent home. At least I lived, I suppose.

"All war is a symptom of man's failure as a thinking animal." - John Steinbeck I dedicate this story to all of the veterans, from Michigan or not, that served our nation and its right to freedom.

About the Author

Eli Ferguson has loved writing since he was in middle school, fostered by his mother, Jen, who works as an ELA teacher. He loves various creative activities, from writing fictional but realistic medieval stories to creating games about alternate history and politics. He also loves reading, specifically about real-world history like World War I, World War II, and the Napoleonic Era; however, despite his love for writing about the Medieval era, he refuses to read fantasy.

Teen Published Finalist

The People Beside You
Jordan Fletcher

The following story contains themes of suicide and may be distressing to some readers. If you or someone you know is struggling with thoughts of suicide, please reach out to a mental health professional or contact the Suicide and Crisis Lifeline at 988 for support.

The sound of soft beeping and a gentle voice woke the man from a drifting sleep. His weary eyes blinked open, prickling as they adjusted to the bright lights overhead. A person tapped his hand softly, and he looked over in answer. "There are some people here to see you, Uncle," the doctor told him, her sad eyes brighter than usual. "Can you send them in please...," The man paused for a second to concentrate. He studied her dark hair tied back in a bun, heart-shaped face, and the kind pair of hazel eyes that were burned into his mind with familiarity. "Tess." He smiled. As of late, most names and faces were harder to grasp, but he knew this one with solid surety. The woman managed a small smile back, then turned away sharply to try and hide the tears welling up in her eyes. "I'll let them in," she said, her voice quivering slightly. "Thank you." The man waited patiently for the doctor to return. It was true he was nearly out of time, but he knew that he had lived life exactly the way they would have wanted. With no regrets.

***

Edward was ready. Or in a way accepting. Accepting that this was his only option. It was his only escape from the constant loneliness that hollowed him out almost entirely. Just enough to make him feel dead without actually being it. Day in and day out. The same feeling repeated over and over. An unrelenting pain that eclipsed everything else. His hands gripped the rope tighter, digging into the frayed strings until the patterns were etched onto his skin. He was scared. So scared. Of the death that awaited him and the people that didn't need him. That never needed him. A silent tear rolled down his cheek and it hit him again. Like an echo resounding through an empty cavern, the loneliness spiraled deeper and deeper until it felt as though his entire body was screaming. It was the final straw. The thing that hardened his resolve as he slipped the loop around his neck. The thing that solidified his defeat. His yield to the opponent he fought every day. And with that final note, he took his final step. Into another reality. Edward felt himself stumble, and the weight of the rope disappeared. *What?* Both of his eyes flashed open as his hand flew to his neck. The rope wasn't there.

Neither was his bedroom. He looked from side to side, trying to take in his surroundings through the confusion. It was extremely difficult though, when his head felt light as air and his body far too heavy to continue standing. He might have fallen to his knees, but even that felt far away. It was as if he were watching himself through someone else's eyes, not able to fully comprehend it through his own. *Was he dead?* Edward felt dead.

There was no way this could actually be happening. Yet as one of his hands fell on a nearby table for support, he could feel its polished, even surface. It was deathly cold. He thought he heard himself gasp and his hand quickly drew back, knocking a picture frame over as he did so. It hit the carpet with a muffled thud, not loud enough to alert anyone, but it still made him jump. Desperately trying to slow his breathing down to a manageable level, Edward bent down to pick it up. He needed to be more careful. If he was caught in a random house, the owners would certainly think he was a robber. Then he would be in even more trouble. As *if he wasn't in enough already*. Edward thought bitterly. Just when he was finally going to escape all of the things he didn't want to feel, he landed center stage of another problem. The unfairness of it all hit him suddenly, and he gripped the picture frame tighter and tighter. Then a soft sound cut through the silence. His grip loosened. Was it crying? Curiosity compelled him forward, and Edward gently placed the picture frame back onto the table. A part of him felt he should hang back, but he ignored it and silently stood up to creep closer to the noise. Closer to a door, open just enough for him to see who was inside. It was odd, but the first thing he noticed was her hair. A bright, sunny auburn. Or it would have been if it didn't look deflated and dull, pulled up in a halfhearted bun. Panels of light from a half-curtained-off window danced across her pale skin and reflected in her puffy, unblinking eyes. She was curled up, knees held close to her chest. There was also something about her that bothered him, other than the strangeness of it all. It was that nagging feeling that he was missing something important. Before he could figure it out, however, the woman spoke in a quiet voice, raw from crying. "I'm sorry Edward," she choked out, and an eerie chill ran through him. Did she know he was there? "It's all my fault. My fault you died." *What?* Then the realization came to him.

Edward raced back to the picture frame and snatched it up hurriedly.

In the photograph was both him and the woman with auburn hair, smiling as if they were the only ones in the world. Something like fear, panic, or confusion gripped his heart, causing every pulse to feel like an earthquake in his system. But that was nothing compared to what he felt as he looked up. To see the woman, a hundred emotions painted on her stricken face. She must have heard him run back to the picture frame, expecting to see some reasonable explanation for the noise. Not this.

"Edward?" he heard her shaken voice call out. But he was already gone. Fading into nothing. When the darkness lifted, Edward found himself outside. He was sitting on the ground, his shoes half in a muddy puddle. Water quickly soaked through them, and he rushed backward, only to run into something cold and solid behind him. He sucked in a surprised breath and twirled to face the thing, fists clenched. Much to his surprise, his attacker was revealed to be nothing more than a crumbling tombstone.

Not known to be a good omen, but it was nothing deadly either. Edward let out the breath he had been holding in an embarrassed laugh, as he took in his surroundings. The snow must have recently melted because the entire graveyard was an ocean of mud, with the occasional clump of weeds stranded in dirty puddles and withered twigs and leaves floating on its muddy surface. The depressing scene was only made worse by weathered tombstones and the inescapable dryness that clung to the air, like a leech attached too long that even salt couldn't deter. He was definitely somewhere new and he wasn't dreaming. *It happened again?* He thought to himself in disbelief. The fact that he had been teleported not once, but twice seemed impossible. Edward needed to escape this all, and fast. Pulling himself upright, he surveyed the graveyard, only for his eyes to land on two figures heading in his direction. Edward wasted no time in retreating behind the tombstone, his mind racing with the fear of being caught. Caught for what he didn't know, but something told him that hiding was his safest option. So he waited a few anxious seconds before eventually mustering up the courage to peek his head out from behind his hiding spot. The pair had stopped at a nearby grave and were now close enough for Edward to discern their features. One of the two was a little girl, with long, brown hair and sad, hazel eyes. The other was a tired-looking man closer to thirty. Neither of them noticed Edward as they stood in a still silence, though the girl was fighting back tears. She tugged on the man's sleeve. "Daddy. Please tell me he's coming back. I want Uncle Edward back." She cried, blocked tears spilling out in a rush. Her father kneeled to hug her and she collapsed in his arms, as he did in hers. "I'm sorry, Tess. I'm sorry." Edward watched everything. He watched the family kneel in the mud, holding on to each other, delicate as glass. They were there for a long time until finally, the little girl let go to dig in her coat pocket. Her small hands, pink from the cold, pulled out a half-crushed wildflower. She hesitated, then gently placed the delicate flower on the tombstone's rough top. The girl's hand rested there for a moment before her father gently took it in his own and slowly led her away. As soon as they turned their backs Edward scrambled over to the grave. His breath caught as he stared, shocked at the freshly carved name. Edward. Tom. Peterson. He backed away from it as if the space would somehow make it less real. He was dead here too. And those people knew him? Edward turned to see the father and daughter, who had stopped to take one last look at the grave. Instead, they saw the man whom they had been grieving only minutes ago. He saw their eyes go wide, just before the wind blew in, strong and cold. Then he was gone. Edward opened his eyes again, for the third time. Sharp sights and smells cut through the hospital room, blinding him with their intensity. The transition from places left him with a resounding headache and even more confusion. He put a hand to his head and leaned back, caught by the chair's wooden backing. Then he took a moment to just sit there. It must have only been half an hour since he had been in his room, yet it felt like everything had changed since then.

He couldn't remember a time when he had felt so unsure. The places he was brought to left him hesitating. And questioning. If he ever got back to his world, reality, apartment, or whatever it was, what would he do when he got there? Or more likely, what would happen? There was no magical answer to his question or some otherworldly sign. All he could do right now was face this reality. But as he stood up, what he faced instead was a hospital bed, and a familiar person lying on it. Hearing his name said by people he didn't know and seeing it on a grave had scared Edward more than he had realized. Even though he had not hours ago tried to hang himself, seeing the pain that death left behind firsthand— even if it was pain caused by another version of him— killed him inside. And now he was having doubts. Doubts about whether or not killing himself would make things better.

Even though he didn't have anyone who would care, these people here were real and the grief he had seen, heavy on their shoulders, was real too.

This realization had slowly been dawning on him but only now had it fully caught up to him as he looked down at himself. There he was. A twenty-ish version of himself yes, but still, it was him. It was Edward, attached to an IV along with several other machines. Edward, whose skin was deathly pale and beaded with perspiration as he fought for his last moments of life. Real Edward wasn't sure how he was supposed to comprehend this. It was like looking into a mirror, only to have your reflection's pose different from yours. Edward told himself he should go. He should look for clues or a way out. Even so, he stood there in a shocked silence for who knows how long, until he caught the faint sound of voices drifting beneath the door.

Reluctantly, he pulled himself away from the bed, and closer to the noise to listen. "Is he going to be okay?" The muffled tone of a woman came from the hallway. "I'm sorry." A man this time, his voice low. "He might hold on for another day or two but that's the best we can manage." "Are you sure there isn't anything you can do? Anything?" The new person said desperately. "I'm sorry," the doctor repeated, "Maybe if we had gotten to him sooner. But now it's too late." Choking sobs followed and mixed like a melancholy band as the doctor took his leave, promising to return in a few minutes. Edward stayed and forced himself to listen to each heartfelt sob. *Why?* In a place where people actually cared about him, why did he always die? It felt hopelessly unfair. Much more unfair than the childish feelings of self-pity that he had felt earlier. Meanwhile, the sniffling outside continued until someone choked out, "It was our fault. He was helping us so much that he wasn't worrying about himself. And we were too happy to notice." The others didn't say anything in response, Edward noticed, but they didn't deny it either. No one spoke up for a few moments until another person joined in. "I don't care if we aren't supposed to see him. I couldn't live with myself if he died alone. I- I already can't, but I know he would be disappointed if I didn't continue with life." "I agree with Max. We all started this together, so we should finish it together too." Edward didn't register that they were all coming in until it was too late and the door was already swinging open. He nearly fell backward with surprise as three people rushed into the small room. A woman with midnight blue eyes, a man with dark brown, and another young man whose eyes held a swampy hue. And every. Single. One. Of those eyes met Edward's, one haunted expression after another. Then he was gone. A fog melting underneath the morning sun. Edward couldn't count all of the realities he saw after that. There were so many, all of them different from each other. Different people.

Different places. Yet all of them included his death and someone seeing him just as he disappeared. He opened his eyes so many times that when he did for the final reality he thought he knew what to expect. This time, however, there was a grassy plain bathed in fog. Faint, drifting sunbeams shone through occasionally, but for the most part, it was peacefully dark.

Then someone stepped forward, into view. It was the first version of him that Edward had seen. Caught mid-smile in a photograph. He was smiling now too, but this one held a deep sadness that wasn't there before as well as... acceptance? He wanted to say so many things, but the only question that came out was, "What happened?" "A robber. He broke into our house with a gun. I knew my fiance was going to try and stop him. So I did it before her. I paid for it with a bullet, but the thief did too." Another Edward walked out from the fog. This one in his early thirties. "My best friend had a daughter. I was watching her as she ran into the street. The car was going to hit one of us, so I chose for her." As he finished, the third Edward stepped up. "My three friends. We were all working hard to open our business. I didn't think anything of being sick, but the disease finally caught up to me."

Other shadows of himself stepped forward until Edward was surrounded by all of the people whose deaths he had witnessed. The first version took a step closer. "We all had someone or someones who needed us. Who were always there with us. You didn't have anyone then but you will soon. And you have all of us right now. We need you, Edward. No one else. We need you to live the life that we never could. To live a life that you can look back on with no regrets. Do you understand?" Edward. Himself. He felt the tears that he had been holding back through everything come pouring out of him. The piece of him that had been missing. The hole that it left was where the loneliness had started. Where it festered. Deep and dark. Because being alone slowly carves out everything. All of the thoughts, emotions, and victories. Because what's the point if you have no one to share them with? Only, now, he finally had the reassurance that he would. That he did.

"I understand." When Edward opened his eyes again he was laying on his back. The noose was still around his neck, but it wasn't choking him like it had been before. And the rough edges of the carpet dug into his skin, as he looked up at the severed rope above him.

43 Years Later

An enormous gathering of people filled the graveyard. Some of them wore black and others didn't. They all knew that Edward wouldn't have cared. He never did as long as everyone was happy. Edward had lived a long 61 years, longer than most with his sickness did. It still felt too short.

Especially for someone who had impacted so many people. Who had changed countless lives. Among them were a loving wife and the family they had made together, the father and daughter whom he had stood with through thick and thin, the friends whom he had built a successful business with, and so many more. And every single one of those people stood beside Edward, as he had stood beside them, ensuring that in his final moments, he was never alone.

About the Author

Jordan Fletcher is currently a freshman at Forest Hills Central High School.

Teen Published Finalist

High School House-Hunters
Katelyn Messina

I never planned to go house-hunting in my junior year. But now, on the last day of school before Christmas break, I find myself in a graveyard of dilapidated houses, ankle-deep in frigid snow, holding a camera.

Just to be clear, this was all *Wes's* idea.

Unfazed by the eerie atmosphere, he leads the way down the snowy path, looking around like he's admiring a fairy village rather than the crooked rows of tumbledown homesteads. A brisk wind whistles between the buildings, and the overcast sky grows gloomier each second, heralding the coming night.

Clenching my camera tighter, I jog to catch up to him and Nick, who have halted a few yards away.

"Alright, listen up." Wes faces us like a drill sergeant addressing his recruits.

"Here's the plan: we film a little bit out here, then we go to the town founder's house for the rest." He points to the looming gate, the entrance to the oldest property in our city, at the end of the path, where the town founder lived seventy-four years ago.

"Are you sure this is a good idea?" I ask.

Wes frowns. "Of course, it is," he answers dismissively. "Now, come on! No time to waste."

He departs, headed for the nearest house, but I remain where I am, fidgeting with my camera, while Nick stoops to retie his boot.

"Hey." Nick nudges my shin with his elbow and glances up at me with a gentle smile. "Stop worrying."

"Not likely," I say. His smile widens, but he doesn't press further.

"Come on, people!" Wes calls. He's already in position by the house, his arms crossed and his foot tapping in the snow. "Not getting any younger over here. Got that camera ready, Kat?"

"Y-yes," I stammer. Nick and I trudge over, and I aim the lens at Wes, my finger poised over the "record" button. "Whenever you're ready."

"Action!" Wes whoops, launching into his introductory spiel. I follow him with the camera as he describes our location, which he dubs the "house graveyard."

Of our troupe, I have the easiest job. While the boys present their points, I stand behind the video camera and film. Easy-peasy. Yet my nerves remain. The last thing I want to do today is stand in this rundown community as night falls, shooting a documentary for our local history class on the day our group project is due. I'm still unsure how we managed to procrastinate until now, and how we were so desperate to find a historic site for our assignment that we settled on this nightmare of a neighborhood.

This is certainly Byerne Harbor's most historic site. It's also the sort of place where serial killers would bide their time, waiting for the right moment to commit mass murder.

"Cut!" Wes declares, breaking my train of thought. I've barely lowered the camera when Wes announces, "Your turn, Nicholas."

Nick grins and assumes Wes's position; when he nods, I press record, filming him as he elaborates on the houses' stories.

"In 1945, just after the settlement of Byerne Harbor, town founder Terrance Moore discovered a treasure buried in the nearby woods." He motions to the spindly treetops behind the mass of dwellings. "He used part of the prize to fund the building of this neighborhood, but the rest he hid away for himself.

According to local lore, he stored the treasure in the cellar of his mansion, but many searches have been made there, to no avail."

He finishes, and when I press "stop," Wes gives an odd laugh beside me.

"Imagine we find the treasure," he says as Nick rejoins us. "We'd be rich! And we'd get an *A*."

"No way we're going to find it," I say. "It's been lost for decades." Wes snorts. "Dibs on holding it in the video."

I roll my eyes. Nick shakes his head.

Wes just forges ahead. "Tally ho, slowpokes! Daylight's a-wasting."

"It's a-wasting, alright," I mutter. Deep shadows are creeping in around the edges of the neighborhood. I stick close to Nick's side as we follow Wes toward the founder's homestead. Towering over the road, the mansion's gate blocks our path, rusty and jagged, with no way to climb over. A padlock as wide as my camera holds the entry shut.

"Darn," Wes murmurs, turning the lock thoughtfully. "Can anybody pick locks?" "Unfortunately, no," Nick says.

I see my opportunity. "Oh, well. Maybe we should just head home. It's getting dark, the gate is obviously locked, and are those footsteps I hear—"

"Got it!" Wes declares. He slams the padlock into the gate with a resounding *clang!* and the corroded lock falls into the snow. Triumphantly, he kicks the gateway open and bursts into the courtyard.

I stand with my mouth slightly open, shocked by the turn of events.

"So...I'm guessing that's a no on going home?" I say weakly.

Nick shrugs sympathetically. "If we turn back now, we'll fail the project."

Then he follows Wes into the estate. With no other options, I trail after.

"Are you sure about this?" I struggle to keep up with them in the thick, clumpy snow.

"Absolutely," Wes responds. He stands near the porch, waiting for Nick and me.

I shiver again, clutching my camera for dear life. "Yep, it's official," I hiss. "We're all going to die."

The manor looms against the darkening December sky. It boasts splintered windowpanes, rotting shutters, a sagging roof, crumbling columns, and a gaping hole in the wall above the porch. Scraggly bushes and leafless trees line the circular driveway and the front walk.

"It's like a real-life haunted house," I breathe. I'm just waiting for someone to jump out and try to violently remove my head from my shoulders with a massive broadsword—or a cumbersome stick.

"Make sure to get me walking in," Wes orders. He and Nick have pulled out their phone flashlights, and the bright beams illuminate large animal tracks in the grimy snow. I whimper.

"Are you—"

"RECORD already," Wes interrupts.

Glaring at him, I level the camera and start filming. Like a king parading through the streets of his kingdom, Wes bounds up the front steps and onto the rickety porch. It moans beneath his weight and visibly bends, but he doesn't notice, instead bragging about how he's about to enter the town founder's home. Then, he barges in, Nick and me following much more carefully.

The estate is just as terrifying inside as outside. Just past the doorway, a broad, decaying staircase leads to the upper floor, and a hall on the left wall leads to the back section of the house. The grey wallpaper is peeling, and the empty picture frames hold images that have long since disintegrated.

"This is awesome," Wes laughs, shining his flashlight around the foyer.

For such an enormous house, the entry is awfully claustrophobic. The two phone lights brighten the entire space, but their glows are hardly comforting; they reveal cobwebs in the corners and insects that scamper across the walls.

"Not sure awesome is the word I'd use," I say, following Wes with the camera.

"It's very…historic," Nick comments, cracking the slightest smile.

"This way, guys!" Wes sets off down the hall. Before he follows, Nick glances curiously back my way, but I shake my head, rejecting his concern. Frankly, I want to turn around and march right back home…but I shake in my boots imagining the solo journey through the dark house graveyard.

So, I start down the hallway, my imagination conjuring all the things that could be lurking in this huge, scary house.

"This—this could be fun!" I try to convince myself. But the hallway is cramped. Only a dim light at the end, where the boys are, illumines my way.

When I emerge behind Nick into the back of the house, I see spider webs covering everything: the wobbly dining set, rusted woodstove, and moldy cupboards. The cracked windowpane on the wall to the left lets in a frosty draft.

On the far wall, two doors lead into an even deeper blackness.

"Oh, dear," I sigh. "We're all gonna—"

"BOO!"

Hands clamp down on my shoulders. I release my camera and scream so loudly that Nick drops his phone.

Wes appears in my peripheral vision, laughing hysterically. Nick looks as startled as I feel as he stoops to retrieve his device.

"You idiot!" I round on Wes. "What was that for?" "You—never saw—it coming—" he gasps, doubling over.

Without even thinking, I slap him soundly in the face. He stops laughing, lifts a hand to his reddening face, and stares at me in astonishment. I, however, have moved on to bigger problems.

Gingerly, I lift my camera from the floor, anticipating the damage. I groan.

It's worse than I thought. I study the fracture, too large to repair, that splits the lens, then I glower at Wes, who's wandered over by Nick. He eyes me warily now, with a new respect. If I wasn't so worried about the camera, I might feel satisfied at that.

"Can you fix it?" Nick asks.

I scoff. "No. We're down a device, gents."

Nick groans. "What now?"

"I don't know," I say, each word dripping with bitter sarcasm. "Ask your valiant leader." Wes frowns and opens his mouth to defend himself, but Nick interjects. "Guys, now is not the time for arguing. We're losing daylight hours."

I cling to my shattered camera tighter as I stand. "Let's just go home."

"Um, hello?" Wes has regained his confidence, and now he climbs atop the wobbly table.

He strikes a power pose, brandishes his phone, and smirks. "We are not going home. Good thing we have these gadgets." He hands the device to Nick and nods his head in my direction. Nick raises his eyebrows but says nothing as he passes me the phone. "Film me up here, Kat."

I set my camera on the ground beside me and open Wes's phone a little more aggressively than needed. I've had it with his shenanigans, but the quicker I film him, the quicker we can go home.

When I start filming, Wes begins a new rant, mixing his own crazy opinions into the fun facts. He orders "cut" a few minutes later, then jumps down from the tabletop. I swear the floorboards buckle under his weight.

"I'm going to try this room while you film Nick," he says, pointing to the nearest doorway. "Don't mind me."

"Need a light?" Nick wonders.

"Please. I'll be fine."

I glance uneasily toward Nick, but he doesn't seem concerned.

Nonetheless, I can't shake the uneasy feeling roiling in my stomach.

In the background of Nick's animated speech, I hear the creaking of Wes's feet on the floorboards and his soft exclamations of amazement. Nick has nearly finished his presentation when—CRASH—BANG—

And a cry of surprise.

Nick and I turn, horrified, to the gaping doorway. Only an eerie silence ensues from beyond. No more squeaking floorboards. No more astounded comments.

"Wes?" Nick shines his phone flashlight at the door.

No answer. I gasp and cover my mouth with shaking hands.

With grim determination, Nick ventures into the room. I linger by the table, shaking uncontrollably from head to toe.

More silence. Then a phone rings. And a voice over speaker phone says, "911. What's your emergency?"

I can't bear it. Gathering my courage, I raise my flashlight and enter the room where my friends disappeared.

The space is small and dark. Nick stands at the edge of a gaping hole in the floor, talking with the 911 operator. His voice is level, but he's trembling as badly as I am. As I approach, he lifts an arm, signaling me to stay back.

When he hangs up, I immediately ask, "What happened? Where's Wes? Is he—"

"Wes is hurt," he explains. "Broke something."

"He's down there?" I peer into the pit.

"Yep."

"Are we going to go save him?"

"Still trying to figure out how." Nick narrows his eyes and flashes his phone light around the room, illuminating a rickety bedframe, a pile of boxes, and...a door.

As Nick investigates the new find, I peek into the hole again. From the glow of my flashlight, I make out the crumpled form below. "Wes?"

"Kat," he answers. He laughs feebly and tries to wave. Blood coats his fingertips. I want to scream. Or throw up. Or both at once.

"Help is coming," Nick calls. "Hang tight." He yanks on the doorknob, and the mysterious door swings open with a sickening crack.

"I'm going down," Nick says, glancing back at me. "You coming?"

"Down?" I repeat. His words compute, and my mouth falls open. "Down there?" "Mm-hmm." Nick lowers a foot past the doorway, onto what must be a staircase.

"There's got to be something that can help."

After a moment of indecision, I creep over to the doorway. Uncertain, I wait at the top of the unsteady staircase while he sets off, testing each step.

"I'm going to die!" I assert.

"You'll be fine," Nick shoots back.

I moan and tentatively lower my foot onto the first stair. Then the next. Our progress is slow and unnerving, but I concentrate on placing my feet exactly where Nick does until I reach the rough basement floor.

Mounds of junk line every wall in a haphazard jumble. In the middle of the room, Wes sits amidst a pile of rubble. Cautiously, I approach him, while Nick searches the mounds.

Wes's leg rests at an unnatural angle, but despite his injury, he beams eagerly. "Welcome to the basement!" he says, gesturing broadly. I catch his slight grimace of pain.

"You say that like it's a good thing."

"It most certainly is." Wes winks. "Have you seen the place?"

I shine my flashlight at the heaps of assorted items.

"Dark, scary, and messy. Like the rest of this darn house."

Wes laughs, but a sudden clatter on the far side of the room grabs our attention. Both of us turn to see what's the matter—then Nick pipes up, "Hey, guys? You have to see this."

I pick my way over to him through the debris and find him shining his flashlight into a cubbyhole in the wall. The light glints off something metallic. "What is it?" I say.

"One way to find out." Nick hands me his phone, then reaches into the hole and grasps the item. With a massive heave, he drags the metallic item out of the cubbyhole, revealing—

"No way," I whisper. Stunned, I open Wes's phone camera and press "record" as Nick unlocks an enormous mahogany chest filled to the brim with gold, silver, and copper coins; strings of pearls; precious gemstones; and myriads of other rarities.

"Yes!" Wes crows, pumping his fists in the air. "I KNEW we'd find it!"

"How did we—but no one—" I fumble.

"The paneling is rotten now. Probably wasn't then," Nick says with a shrug. "But I bumped it, and it opened."

"Ha, we're rich!" Wes shouts.

Nick frowns. "This'll hardly cover your medical bill."

He and I laugh, while Wes protests. We rejoice over our discovery until sirens blare outside the house. The next moments pass in a blur of flashing lights, movement, and questions. EMTs prepare to move Wes out on a stretcher.

A police officer with a bushy mustache interrogates Nick and me on how we got into the house, what we were doing, and how Wes managed to fall.

Our parents arrive and demand to know why on earth we thought it a good idea to come here alone at night. My mom sentences me to a life grounding.

My dad complains about my broken camera.

But once the initial irritation of the moment passes, everyone notices the treasure. And they pepper us with more questions. We don't have all the answers—and the boys look as exhausted as I feel.

Before the EMTs and our guardians usher us all out of the house, Wes cries, "Wait!"

After explaining his plan to the doctors, he orders me to hand my phone to my mom, then asks the EMTs to drag the chest closer to him and calls Nick and me over, while he grabs fistfuls of his precious discovery.

The camera snaps, the EMTs rush Wes to the nearest hospital, and the parents fuss over Nick and me and parade us home. Every moment, my eyelids droop lower and lower, until my head finally hits the pillow and I'm home—safe and sound, far away from the house graveyard.

"Did we get an A?"

After everything we've been through, the question is so stupid that I laugh out loud.

"Yes, we got an A," I assure Wes.

He grins at me from his hospital bed. Three days after his accident, he's back to his lively self. "My part of the documentary was the best," he insists.

"What, the part where you fell through the floor and almost died?" Nick says.

"Pfft. I knew what I was doing." Wes waves a dismissive hand. "We wouldn't have found the treasure otherwise."

"City council did love us for that," Nick agrees. "Maybe they'll name a park bench in your honor."

Wes beams, but then he looks abashed. "I owe you both an apology." He glances up at me "Especially you, Kat. Sorry for not believing you...and for breaking your camera."

"Hey. Cameras can be replaced," I say. "Best friends can't."

"Moral of the story: always trust a woman," Nick jokes, ruffling my hair.

"Glad we're finally in agreement, gents," I tease. I pull a Sharpie from my pocket, crouch beside Wes and scrawl my name on his cast. "No hard feelings."

Nick signs his name, as well. Then he frowns pensively. "One more thing, Wes," he adds. "No more adventures." We laugh, then Wes nods.

"Okay, sure," he concedes, casting me a knowing look. "No more adventures."

About the Author

Born and raised in the metro Detroit area, Katelyn Messina has always had a passion for writing. From the moment she could hold a pencil properly, she dedicated herself to authoring everything from haiku to novels; what started as an idle hobby has become an obsession with concocting plotlines, building worlds, and developing characters. When not carefully crafting narratives, Katelyn slaves over schoolwork, slings chicken sandwiches at her local Chick-fil-A, sings low notes, and spends time with her friends and family. It's these loved ones, and the adventures she has with them, that have inspired many of her book concepts and many of her valiant heroes and heroines, including the dynamic trio in "High School House-Hunters". It's her dream to one day make this hobby her career—and to share the stories trapped inside her with the world.

Teen Published Finalist

I Will Always Eat Burnt Biscuits
Lucy Yoder

The kitchen hummed with a sort of diminished, bothered wail.

Of course, I immediately recognized the source of the pitchy sound: my baby sister, Jessie, was huffing from her highchair, a spread of mushy peas flaking her face. Jessie started banging the table of her highchair, causing her strawberry-flavored baby puffs to ricochet through the air.

My mother abandoned her attempt at biscuit-making, consoling my sister's petulant whines before they escalated into a vexed tantrum.

"Shhh." I heard my mother whisper into my sister's ear from the kitchen table. Ever since I had started fourth grade, the amount of homework I had every night suddenly swelled to the point where I had to multitask: long division while consuming wilted bits of Caesar salad, vocabulary practice while stuffing impressive amounts of curried sausage down my throat, or—as of this night—attempting to tear through tough bits of meatloaf while blocking out Jessie's surging fits.

Jessie's howls reverberated across the room, causing a tested nerve in my forehead to pulse with pain.

I whipped my head over to my mother, who was bouncing Jessie up and down while transferring the pan of homemade biscuits she had been working on to the interior of the blazing oven. Even from the far corner of the room, I swear I felt a faint lick of heat flare across my face, heating my insides against the cold drear of rain that sloshed outside.

I blew a breath of hot air, my bangs fluttering across my forehead.

Reaching into the depths of my Jansport backpack, I yanked out the torn and tussled pages of my social studies folder; the blue, paper pockets were folded and warped with being constantly stuffed into my bag.

My teacher had assigned us a project where we had to pick a period of history and recreate a picture book on it using the non-fiction section of the library. While I was sorting through the dusty tomes and worn books in the library, I saw a text regarding the Civil War. My dad mentioned the Civil War once, and it was the only topic that I was vaguely keen on, so I snatched the book off of the shelf to use on my project.

I grabbed my plastic container of pens, gluesticks, and markers, popping the neon lid of the gluestick off to attach a picture of Abraham Lincoln to the glossary page.

The dim, incandescent glow of the kitchen lamp illuminated above me, causing my attention to wane with yet another distraction. Jessie had hushed a bit—her snuffly sobs were interrupted only by my mother's faint hum.

I recognized the song immediately. The morose, melancholy rhythm with a lilt of bittersweet reflections. My dad always cranked the volume on the radio up whenever the local station chose to play it. If my mother was present, he would scoop her into his arms regardless of her protests, belting every line with the might that only a balding middle-aged father of two young daughters could muster:

> *Nightswimming, remembering that night*
> *September's coming soon*
> *I'm pining for the moon*
> *And what if there were two*
> *Side by side in orbit*
> *Around the fairest sun?*
> *That bright, tight forever drum*
> *Could not describe nightswimming.*

Even R.E.M.'s brilliant vocals would be drowned out by the tenderness in my dad's voice.

Once I pasted Abraham Lincoln's cutout head onto the paper pages of my Civil War booklet, I started tracing a map of the United States to label each of the states and their relative allegiance to the Union.

My mother brushed by, her humming swelling as she reached the chorus of the song. Jessie bumped along in her arms, her chunky baby face tear-strewn and somber.

"Are you all done with your dinner, Emily?" My mother asked me, cradling Jessie on her hip in order to clear my plate away. I didn't make eye contact with her; instead, I started directly ahead into the backsplash, a latticework of greens arranged in a hexagonal pattern. Above the backsplash were the hand-painted ceramic spice jars, each of them labeled with fun words like 'basil,' or 'bay leaves.'

"The meatloaf was dry," I simply muttered, noticing how her eye caught the mound of untouched food that lingered on my plate.

My mother sighed, setting the plate into the sink with a faint clatter. She then proceeded to place a kettle of water on the stovetop, preparing to make an evening tea before my dad arrived home from work.

"Well," she said, "you could have added some ketchup to help the texture. That is what I always used to do when Grandma made something inedible—douse it with ketchup."

A roil of frustration slinked through my stomach.

"Well, maybe next time you can actually try and make something edible. And, for the record, meatloaf is gross even with a bottle of ketchup added to it," I responded, cocking my head slightly as I outlined the United States in a big, fat black marker.

The rain was the only thing to answer me, a thrumming patter against the roof.

After a few moments, I lifted my head to my mother's figure: the fingers on her left hand were pinching the upper bridge of her nose, warding off some sort of ache while her right hand cradled Jessie.

She inhaled. Exhaled. Lifted her head slightly, waves of lustrous hair sliding off her shoulders.

"I'm going to put Jessie down for bed. If your dad gets back from work while I am in there, please—" She swung Jessie around, carrying her with two arms. "Please just be nice to him."

"Whatever."

My mother disappeared with a sputtering Jessie, leaving me alone with the pattering drizzle and my sticky Civil War booklet. A few minutes passed by before the brassy hum of boiling water from the old stove gurgled in the distance.

From the back door leading from the garage, I heard the entry swing open. A scented flurry of leaves, rain, and gale battered my nose, accompanied by the nearing scent of my dad's cologne as he kicked his work shoes off and appeared in the kitchen.

Adhering to my mother's pleas, I lifted my head from my homework to offer him a faint, tight-lipped smile. I was quite vexed: all I wanted was a moment with no distractions—no rain, no wailing little sisters, and no hissing tea kettle.

My dad's face was rather wan, the paleness induced simply by the stress and tedium of his office job. His hair, thin and straw brown, black-and-blue striped tie, crinkled white shirt with a coffee-stained collar—all of it glared back at me as I tried to do my work.

"Hey, M&M," he said, dropping his leather work bag on a kitchen chair and embracing me from above. He planted a kiss on the top of my mousy hair, the windswept aroma lingering even as he withdrew. "How was your day?"

He turned to take the blistering kettle off of the stove, digging around the ceramic spice jars for his favorite evening tea: chamomile. He always said it tasted like apples and spring, yet whenever I sipped it, I thought it tasted like a mound of dirt.

"Good," I grumbled. He sat down in the chair next to me, flipping through the haphazard mess of papers that were strewn across the table.

As his chamomile steeped, the scent brewed, stinging my nostrils with the pungent waft of bitter apple and saturated dirt.

"Where's your mama?" He asked, ruffling my hair and turning around in his chair to browse the kitchen, scanning as if my mother would suddenly pop up from behind Jessie's messy highchair.

"Putting Jessie to bed."

Footsteps pattered down the bedroom hallway, and my mother appeared in the kitchen moments later, a smear of spit up mingling with the stain of Jessie's dark tears.

"Hey, darling," my dad said, jolting out of his seat to pull my mother into his arms. She squirmed a bit, mentioning something about cleaning or washing dishes, but he silenced her with a firm kiss. Her eyes softened momentarily after they pulled apart, and he flicked a rogue crumb off of her shirt.

They made eye contact for a moment, a conversation of a thousand words and a lifetime of troubles echoing between them. Suddenly, my mom's head perked up, her eyes losing any sense of safety and comfort.

Her head darted toward the old oven, which had the faint odor of burnt biscuits rolling from the closed door.

"I'm going to go put some sweatpants on, darling," my dad said, turning toward the hall. "There is only so long I can go in tight pants and a stiff shirt."

As he walked away, my mother frantically shoved oven mitts onto her hands, scrunching her nose at the potency of sour, charred biscuits.

"Those look crusty," I commented, craning my head.

Smoke billowed from the oven, little wafts of grey fog making the kitchen all murky and dark. After placing the pan on top of the stove, she cracked open the window above the sink, allowing the musty whirl of rain-soaked night breeze in.

"I hope you know that Dad is going to comment on those." I don't know why I felt the need to continue, to positively berate her biscuit-making efforts. She baked biscuits daily for him—it was just a poor chance that tonight they ended up unattended to.

I don't remember which swear word she uttered at this moment, but I do remember being rather taken aback by the sudden flash of violent language.

The syllable dissipated into the murkiness of the smoke shortly after, followed by my dad's distinct humming as he re-entered the kitchen, clad in cuffed joggers and his college crewneck.

He kissed my mother's head for a brief moment before settling himself at the circular table, flipping through the contents of my Civil War booklet as I referenced a date from a book found deep within the non-fiction section of the school's library.

"I poked my head into Jessie's room," he told my mother. "It looks like she's finally figuring out how to fall asleep."

My mother avoided eye contact as she responded with a tight-lipped, dejected smile. I don't know why, but a surge of satisfaction expanded in my chest: nobody wanted to eat gross food, and it was only reasonable that she felt guilty for screwing up her only job.

Nightswimming, remembering that night
September's coming soon
I'm pining for the moon
And what if there were two
Side by side in orbit
Around the fairest sun?
That bright, tight forever drum
Could not describe nightswimming.

My dad hummed the lyrics to R.E.M.'s "Nightswimming," oblivious to the hunk of brittle meatloaf that was placed in front of him. He was seemingly entranced by the sketches I drew, the facts and figures taped onto the red and blue backdrop—

"Your meatloaf, John," my mother said.

She slid a bottle of ketchup across the table.

"Thank you, darling."

I watched as my mother glanced at the crispy biscuits, the charred exterior still pungent regardless of the cracked window.

I shivered.

She piled the burnt biscuits on the plate and slid them across the table along with the vessel of butter that had been resting on the counter. I held my breath—for some, cold, cruel reason, I wanted my dad to admonish her stupid biscuits.

But he buttered them without a single comment, stuffing them down his mouth along with the bits of nasty, flavorless meatloaf.

He didn't even add ketchup.

"I'll get the dishes, darling," he said once his meatloaf was gone and at least three biscuits were consumed. He had a peaceful, content look on his face, one that seemed to seek oblivion rather than disputation.

She muttered something to him—something probably kind and thoughtful—and brushed her lips to the top of his head. My mother disappeared into the hallway for an early bedtime.

I sat and watched my dad for a few moments. All he did was read the rest of the newspaper from earlier in the morning, humming his song in a carefree beat. He licked his fingers to flip the page. Read, nod thoughtfully.

Heave a tired, loaded sigh. Lick fingers.

He must've caught me staring at him because he set the newspaper on the table and crossed his hands on his lap.

"Anything wrong, M&M?"

I was feely beyond testy, every bone of tolerance in my body aching from being pulled and prodded.

"How come you didn't say anything about the biscuits?" I blurted.

I was ready for my lecture. I was eager for a fight, a moment where my bitter, bottled attitude could finally be released.

But he smiled and leaned forward, ruffling the feathery hair on my head.

"Today at work," he started, gazing at me intently with those tired eyes, "a few very interesting events occurred. You've met Miss Louise, right Em? She's the one who was pregnant with twins the first time you met her. She gave you candy when you visited the building on Halloween."

I nodded, pulling the image of Miss Louise to the forefront of my mind.

Her vibrant red ringlets, the glimmer in her eye as she slipped caramel apple suckers into my Trick-or-Treat bag.

"She's a nice lady. Miss Louise has been out of the building for a while so she could have her babies, but the delivery didn't go quite as she hoped it to. Only one of the babies made it."

A sickly feeling swelled in my stomach, causing a blockage in the areas that were typically very adept at producing sound.

"Miss Louise stopped by to deliver the news. She's very happy and very sad, something I don't expect you to understand because I don't fully understand it myself. Does that make sense, Em?"

I nodded, I think. It did make sense—for her, not for me. It could never make sense for me, the multitude of joy and sadness, heaved together with storms of sorrow and brilliant rainbows.

"Miss Louise gave all of her co-workers peanut butter cookies before she left the building."

"Peanut butter is gross." The only comment I could manage.

"They were homemade," was all he said before standing up to put his meatloaf plate in the sink. He sat back down and continued.

"After Miss Louise left, we were all very surprised, of course. Very happy for the child but very sad for the other one. I got back to work at my desk." He paused for a moment, the weight on his face growing heavier and heavier, the outside shadows blending in with his darkened emotions.

"You remember my boss, Em? The nice man who always wears fun socks?"

An image of this exact man came to mind. He was bald with a very shiny head, his socks in this particular image a vivid shade of neon beneath the hem of his work pants.

"Mr. Mason," I said.

"Yes, Mr. Mason. A good friend, a good man. He came into my office. He then pointed at a picture I had taped on the wall—" He mimicked the gesture, pointing in the distance. "And he said, 'You have a very nice family, John.' He knew about you and Jessie—and your mother, of course."

"What picture was it?"

"'The picture of us at the hospital after Jessie was born.'"

I smiled, recalling the moment that I touched my little sister for the first time. She was slimy and alien-like, but adorable nonetheless.

"He asked how everyone was doing," my dad continued, explaining with his hands as he went. "Asked about Jessie, your mother, and you."

"Why?"

"He's a nice man, Em."

"But why are you telling me this?" I asked. I was touched by Miss Louise's story, but I didn't understand how either of them tied to—

"He said that the company is relocating to a different city across the country and that I have two choices: stay or leave. Move with the firm—or quit altogether."

I think that the rain even jolted in shock, sending a tremor of silence through the kitchen. My mouth was dry, and it had nothing to do with the meatloaf or the crisp aroma of biscuits.

"Are we going to move?" My voice, once filled with a pugnacious edge, one that sought resolution through quarrels, suddenly sounded beyond my age—mature yet young, rid of the insufferable testiness that echoed earlier.

"I don't know yet, Em. I don't know," was all my dad said, placing his head in his hands. There was a little, dainty pause. Fragile and scary.

"Is that why you didn't yell at Mom about the biscuits? You were thinking about Miss Louise and Mr. Mason?" I asked, picking at bits of dried glue on my project. I feared what I would see in his eyes, the shades of pain that would haunt the heavy lids.

"Something like that. Sometimes a burnt biscuit is simply irrelevant." He paused, and to my surprise, a fleeting smile darted across his face.

"Sometimes it's nice to change things up—it keeps me on my toes."

"But she had one job—"

"She worked very hard today. She is tired, and the last I should do—the last thing anyone should do—is make her worried about something as small as biscuits."

I wanted to cry so badly. Tears were overdue, and the pain only deepened when he stood up and left for his room, leaving me with a messy kitchen, dregs of chamomile tea, and a half-eaten plate of biscuits.

About the Author

Lucy Yoder is in her final year of high school. Although she loves to do anything related to reading and writing, Lucy also enjoys hanging out with her friends and family and creating lifetime memories. Her short story "I Will Always Eat Burnt Biscuits" was written to illustrate life from a child's eyes and highlight the hidden complexities that lie in daily routines.

Youth Judges' Choice Winner

A Long-Forgotten Memory

Leyla Köroğlu

The sun shone brightly through my leaves, dotting the grass with specks of light. It was a warm fall day in late September. My branches creaked and groaned as a breeze swept through the garden. Today felt promising. Lately I've felt so lonely, so unconnected, so unwanted. I 've always felt as though something was missing from my life. The house that I belong to has had a for-sale sign in front of it for months. Now finally, in bold red letters it's marked: **SOLD.** I've been so excited for the day the new owners move in. I can't wait to meet them! I wasn't exactly sad to part with the old owner. He wasn't mean, but he mostly kept to himself. He never came outside, never planted flowers in between my roots. He didn't come sit under my shade in the summer and read a book at dusk, like I wanted him to so badly. And of course, he never swung on my wooden swing. A squirrel named Hazel who lives in my branches knows more about him than I do. She found an opening through the vents and can slip into the house whenever she wants.

She said that he wasn't very exciting, but for Hazel that meant that he didn't keep a giant load of nuts in the pantry. Hazel's babies—Walnut, Chestnut, Peanut, and Macadamia Nut—were in fact playing in my tallest branches at the moment. Well, back to the present. I watched the seemingly endless line of cars driving by, waiting for one to pull into the driveway and to see the new owners.

***

Finally, after what seemed like an eternity, but was most likely only a few minutes, a rusty blue car covered in bumper stickers pulled in. Strangely, one of the stickers stood out to me. It read:

I still haven't found what I'm looking for.

I felt like I had heard that phrase before. Something about it nagged at me like an old, long-forgotten memory. I took it as a good omen that the new owners would be nice.

A tall woman with long, wavy brown hair climbed out of the driver's seat.

She opened the back door, unstrapped a baby from her car seat and lifted her out. A girl who looked to be about twelve years old stepped out of the passenger seat. Two identical girls, I assumed they were twins, fell out of the back, stumbling and tripping over each other as they raced to be the first one to see the new house. They looked like they were nine or ten years old. They were dressed similarly and I could tell it was going to be a while before I could tell them apart.

"Well kids, welcome to our brand-new home!" Something about the mother's voice seemed familiar, though I couldn't quite place what. I am a tree, after all and I have seen and heard a lot of people in my life, so I didn't think much of it. But it still felt like I was forgetting something... The whole family had curly brown hair and matching big brown eyes that seemed familiar and oddly comforting to me. I saw Hazel scamper over to them and then under the car to observe the newcomers from a safe distance. The baby squealed and clapped her hands together with delight and pointed at her.

I smiled inwardly. After all, it's hard to smile when you're a tree.

I was going to like this family!

***

A while later, after the children had explored the house and taken in the moving boxes, which had arrived along with furniture in a large moving van, I learned that there was one last surprise left in store for me: the family had a cat! I couldn't believe my luck. Someone other than a food-oriented squirrel to keep me company! I couldn't wait to meet her.

The next day, after the family had settled in, I acquainted myself with Coco. She walked out of the house and right over to me, tail held up high and a very vain expression on her face.

"Cats," I thought, rolling my eyes inwardly. "Hello tree, I am Coco, the cat." She introduced herself. "I am Maple, the tree," I said, as she climbed up my trunk. "Well, I'm glad we didn't move to an apartment this time, I wouldn't have had any trees to climb!" "This time?" I wondered aloud. "Oh yes, my family has moved far too many times to count. You see the mother, Amber, is a journalist, she enjoys writing very much but every newspaper she has worked for has fired her, rejecting her stories and ideas for every possible reason. It has really discouraged her and it's been really hard for her lately." Coco explained to me. I immediately felt sorry for her, but what could I possibly do? I was just a tree, after all.

***

At the crack of dawn, I awoke to the sound of a voice. I noticed the mother, Amber, out on the porch, with dark circles under her eyes, talking to someone on the phone. "I just don't know what to do. I can't seem to keep a single job, and every time I get fired, it just discourages me even more.

If only my parents were here! To be honest I've felt discouraged since the day I lost them. I haven't gone a day without thinking of them! I feel like I've lost part of myself, losing them!" She buried her face in her hands and wept silently. I knew exactly how she felt.

Alone. Lost. No one to depend on or turn to when times are tough.

Before I could think another thought, I realized that something about her, the way she sat, curled into a ball, her face buried in her hands, how sad she looked, reminded me of something. A long-forgotten memory tucked away, lost over all these years. I wasn't sure what it meant. But I knew one thing for sure.

I wanted to help her so badly, I wanted to comfort her, reach out to her, remind her that she wasn't alone. But what could I do? I was rooted to the ground. I felt hopeless and unnoticed.

Suddenly I heard footsteps. The eldest daughter appeared in the doorway.

When she saw her mom crying, she didn't say anything, but just hugged her, holding her tight, never letting go.

Despite how sad she had just been, Amber managed a weak smile. I felt touched, seeing the act of kindness the daughter had done. "I wish I could do that," I thought sadly. Simply reach out and give her a hug. Still, watching them together made me feel happy like never before.

***

Over the weekend before school started, I got to know the children better.

The eldest, Rose, was sort of like a mother to the younger children when Amber was working. The children spent the weekend mostly underneath me.

They had picnics, tea parties, and endless games of hide and seek, while chatting about everything in the warm September sun. Watching them, being there, most importantly being a part of their games and their fun, made me realize something. It made me realize how much I had missed having the company of children. It made me realize how utterly lonely I had been all these years. How I had felt like no one wanted me, like no one cared about me.

The strange thing was that no child had ever lived in this house before.

At least, not that I could remember. There was the swing though... I had always wondered where it came from. And the children loved it! The twins, Chrysanthemum and Zinnia, spent hours each day taking turns pushing each other on it. I was glad it was finally being put to use.

One day the children noticed the squirrel family and immediately ran inside and brought out a giant load of nuts to feed them with. The squirrel family was delighted. They stuffed their little cheeks full with nuts and set to work cracking more open once they had finished. The children laughed with delight at their funny antics and especially loved the little babies. The twins took turns feeding them and holding them. "Now, now don't spoil them" I said. "Speak for yourself!" Hazel squeaked, though it sounded more like, "Eak fuh urrsuhf!", due to the fact that her cheeks were stuffed with nuts. I laughed, because, well, who wouldn't? Coco, like all cats, just held her head up and harrumphed, but I could tell she thought it was funny, too.

That Sunday evening felt perfect. As the sun set, the children were bathed in a golden haze, laughing, enjoying themselves.

I realized that I, too, was enjoying myself as well for the first time in what seemed like forever. In fact, this weekend was most certainly the most enjoyable one I had had since I could remember!

***

Later that night, Rose went inside with Dahlia, the little pigtailed, one-year-old baby. She was chatting with their mother, who had spent the day working outside on the porch, watching the children out of the corner of her eye while she was writing. After they had gone inside, I overheard a conversation between the twins. "Ugh, mom never has time for us anymore.

It's always Rose who looks after us lately," Chrysanthemum said. "Go easy on her, she's been through a lot. You know what it's like for her right now," Zinnia replied. "I know. But sometimes I wish she had more time to play with us." "Yeah," Chrysanthemum sighed. "Me too." Then they swung on my swing until late into the night, barefoot in the cool grass, everything shrouded in shadows.

As I watched them, I felt a strange connection with their mom.

She'd seen a lot, but she felt as if something was missing from her life.

And honestly, it must be a lot for her right now. She couldn't keep a job, had four children to look after all by herself, no parents to depend on and to turn to. Then, I realized how her children had helped her, how Rose took care of the twins, baby Dahlia, kept them entertained, out of their mother's way, so she could focus on her work. How Rose had come out and just hugged her mom, keeping her close that morning she had been so sad.

***

The next day Rose and the twins went off on their very first day of their new school.

Their mother packed them lunches, kissed them on the head, made sure they had brushed their teeth and wished them good luck. I did, too, as I watched their shoes crunch on the fallen leaves that covered the sidewalk.

They wore brand-new back-to-school clothes and bulky backpacks stuffed with books.

They slowly got smaller and smaller until they disappeared from sight.

***

Later that evening, after Amber had put Dahlia to bed, she walked outside and over to me.

The sky cast golden rays of light through my branches, illuminating the ground around me. The sun was setting, and the sky shone beautiful shades of orange, red and pink, making the garden feel somehow magical, full of hope and possibilities. "What am I going to do with myself?" she sighed hopelessly and looked up at my branches covered in bright red leaves.

Despite her sadness, she smiled. Without thinking, I let a single, fiery red maple leaf flutter down from my tallest branches. It swayed back and forth, riding a breeze before slowly settling in her outstretched palm. She laughed softly in surprise and wonder.

Her laughter, along with just about everything else about her, nagged at my memory. She gently lifted the leaf up to the setting sun, gazing at its beauty.

Then she looked up at me again, a smile illuminating her face. Her familiar face, her smile, the way she laughed, the bumper sticker... Suddenly I remembered everything!

How her parents had planted me with her when she was a little baby and how she had spent her childhood in this very house. How Maple was her very first word as a toddler. How she had played in my shade, all summer long, laughing and swinging in the swing her father had suspended from my branches. *That's where the swing came from!* How she and her mother would listen to the radio together underneath me. And how her mother would chime in and sing her favorite song, "I still haven't found what I'm looking for," whenever it came on.

The horrible day her parents died in the car crash, how she sat for hours next to me, weeping silently, her head buried in her hands, her face in the shadows. How all I wanted to do was make her feel better and remind her she wasn't alone in this world. But alas, she had to move away to live with her aunt and uncle in West Virginia. I remembered her departure, how she had wept and wept when she learned she had to leave me here alone.

Suddenly Amber's eyes filled with tears. She looked up at me and by the look on her face, I knew she remembered everything as well. She threw her arms around my trunk. "Maple? Is it really you? After all this time?" she asked. My branches swayed up and down in the wind. It looked like I was nodding! When Amber saw this her eyes grew round in wonder. Then she cried, "I can't believe it! I remember everything now! It's been so long but we've found each other again at last!" She wept out of pure happiness for a while, hugging me the entire time. I felt warm all over.

All those early memories of mine, long forgotten, were finally brought into the light, noticed, remembered. I finally knew what that lonely empty part of me had longed for all these years. My memories. Amber. My best friend.

***

A few days later, Amber was sitting underneath me, leaning against my trunk, her eyes closed, the breeze tousling her curls back and forth. We both sighed out of happiness. She couldn't hear me of course, but I didn't care. I knew she knew how happy I was, too. Then, she pulled out her little writer's journal and looked up at me.

"You know what Maple?" she asked. "I decided to quit journalism and write novels! I think I'm going to write a story about my life. About us."

She smiled and I smiled, too. Inwardly of course, but I knew she knew. She took a deep breath and opened her journal to a fresh page.

Then she took out a pencil and began to write: *One day, long ago, when I was young, I planted a seed. Now I look up in wonder at what it's become and think about how it's changed my life.* "Wow," I thought. The sense of being unwanted and alone vanished in seconds. "I've never thought about myself that way before..."

About the Author

Leyla Köroğlu is 11 years old and lives in Ann Arbor. She speaks German and Turkish and loves reading and writing. In her free time, she also enjoys drawing, listening to music, and playing with her two cats. She also takes dance classes with her best friends Elka and Grace.

Youth Judges' Choice Runner-Up

Halloween House
Nora Sportel

I sit and wait while I listen to the rat-a-tat-tat of pencils tapping on the tables and scribbling down notes. I listen to the snoring of Mike Wilson, who has his head tilted back and his eyes shut droopily. I guess you can't really blame him, though. I listen to Abby Johnson, who is slurping down her water like a dolphin trying to squeal in the air. And sure, I listen to my teacher, Mrs. Tron, too.

Well, I don't necessarily listen, I guess. I just hear her. I watch her talk in her long, black dress with a tight blue bow wrapped around her waist. Her long, jet-black hair is thrown into a tight bun with one perfectly curled strand hanging down. Sure, I admire her really beautiful hair, but not her attitude. And because of that attitude of hers, I wish I could tell myself I hate her hair just as much as I hate her.

What is her attitude exactly? Well, she always walks around like she owns the school, she always makes us feel bad for our mistakes instead of encouraging us to do better, and often, she likes to embarrass us (or me) in front of the whole class.

I hear her constant high-pitched voice that sounds like a never-ending fire alarm go on and on and on about some sort of war. Or I think that's what she's talking about, because that's what Lily, my best friend, and a straight-A student, tells me we're learning about during recess.

I'm a nice person. I do well getting along with people and everything. I just get distracted really, really easily. But Lily has her own way of teaching, one that I can pay attention to easily. So she tells me what we're learning, and I learn.

I also suppose I often judge people and their things a little more than I probably should, but I don't think that matters very much, because I never tell people what I think about them or show them what I think about them.

I blow a blond curl of hair out of my face, far louder than I intended it to be.

I think Mrs. Tron notices, because she looks over at me, clearly disappointed in what she sees.

"Christy, will you repeat what I just said or show that drawing to the class please?" asks Mrs. Tron. I look down at my sketch of Mrs. Tron with a ruler in her hand and her mouth open and a speech bubble of her saying "History, blah blah war blah blah past blah blah blah..." and I sigh. I have absolutely no idea what we're learning about or what she just said, but if anyone sees this drawing...

Luckily, the bell saves me as it echoes through the room. I jump up and gather my stuff. I rush to the hallway and join the flow of people rushing to get out of the school doors like a firework just waiting to explode, hearing Mrs. Tron mumble something about how disrespectful of a student I am.

Why are we all in such a rush? Great question. The answer is (drum roll please...) Halloween! I was going to go to my house and quickly change into my costume, and then head to Lily's house soon after. Since Lily is new at my school, I haven't had a chance to go to her house yet.

I had other friends last year, in fifth grade. But this year, it's almost like they're too good for me. It's so hard not to be annoyed by them sometimes.

But right now, I'm just so happy about Halloween! Lily and I had picked out our costumes together at a cute local costume store called "Christopher's Costumes" a couple of weeks ago. She's going to be a glass of milk and I'm going to be a cookie. I know, such a good combo. We had spent days brainstorming together until finally we were at my house and my mom offered us some chocolate chip cookies. That was when Lily asked to dip it in a glass of milk.

"That's it!" I had shouted. "One of us should be a cookie, and the other a glass of milk!" I smile at the memory.

I rush to the car line, doubling my average pace, but still following the "no running in the halls" rule of my school. As soon as I shove the doors open, I begin scanning the cars. Finally, I see my navy-blue car about ten vehicles down the line. Normally, I would wait until my mom comes over here, but today I run as fast as I can.

I swing the door open with a swoosh.

"Go, go, go!" I shout to my mom enthusiastically, who is wearing a black sweater over a long, lavender-colored dress, so I assume she just got home from work.

She smiles slightly.

"We still have to wait through the line, Christy," she notes in her calm, sweet tone of voice. She's always like this. I'd never heard her yell. Ever.

Well, except for the time we were at a store that sold rocks and gems and crystals, and I broke a huge crystal that cost over 1000 dollars, and she had to pay for it.

I sigh heavily. She's right. I still have to wait in the car line. I also realize it doesn't do much that I ran because I'm not going to Lily's house until 5:30, so it'll still be a couple of hours before we go to her house.

"How was your day?" asks my mom. I think about it for a second.

"It was longer than usual," I finally tell her. "I just can't wait!"

After that, we're silent enough to hear a pin drop. I watch the houses roll by. Sometimes, I like to imagine which one I might move into in the future. There is one that's very neon chartreuse with a vibrant red door and sky blue shutters.

"Never. Not in a million years," I think to myself. But there is one that grabs my attention even more than a rainbow house ever could. It's a small house with black and blue bricks. It's placed on the end of an old alley, there are dead roots growing up along the crumbling and cracked walls with a couple dead trees surrounding the house.

I shudder. And on Halloween, out of all days…

I do my best to ignore it. It's Halloween, after all! Last year, I got a giant Twix bar, my favorite! I still remember biting into the soft chocolate and through the satisfying crunch and right down into the middle of the smooth, sticky caramel.

My mouth starts watering at the thought of it.

But I keep remembering that house…

Finally, we get home. I hope that walking around a little and the excitement of my costume will distract me from the house that keeps making my stomach knot up, making it impossible to breathe and my hands turn itchy red and I then I feel beads of sweat coming on my forehead and—

I pause and catch myself. I take a deep breath.

"Think of something else," I tell myself.

I look around. It seems like my dad hasn't gotten home from work yet.

He works at a restaurant and sometimes gets home by lunch and sometimes not until 8:00 pm. It changes each day. But the terrible house…

Quickly, I run to my room and grab my round, chocolate chip cookie costume to distract myself. It goes right over my head and onto my shoulders.

It has a bite-shaped dent at the top right of it, and it's made out of soft, cottony fabric. I really can't wait!

I sprint up the stairs. My mom has already seen my costume, but it's different on actual Halloween day! She has me pose for a couple of photos, I have a snack, read a little, and before I know it, it's time to go!

I hurry to the car and we start heading to Lily's house. I watch the houses roll by out the window and try really hard not to think about the house, but instead about my fun costume! I haven't seen Lily in hers yet, so I imagine what she would look like as a glass of milk. I chuckle as an image of a glass of milk with long hair and eyes pops into my head.

In 200 meters, turn right and head down Glummowl avenue, said the GPS voice. "Glummowl?" I think. I shudder. Halloween had never been like this before. Never so... spooky.

But then I see my mom turn onto Glummowl avenue.

"Time to get out!" she says enthusiastically.

But I see it, right out the window, and then everything goes black.

"Christy!" says a muffled voice. My eyes flutter open to the blurry sight of my mom looking down at me. I realize that I'm breathing really fast, and I'm really hot and sweaty.

"Did I actually *faint?*" I wonder. "I haven't ever fainted before, but that house is really scary, and it's the only house on this alley, but that can't be where Lily lives, but, but..." I take a few deep breaths and finally speak to my mom.

"Mom, that's not Lily's house," I tell her firmly but shakily.

"What do you mean? Of course it is. Let's just go ahead and knock, and we can see what happens," she responds. I sigh. I know I'm not going to get out of going with her, so I reluctantly agree.

I get out of the car and drag my feet as I walk slowly towards the door.

My mom sighs, but doesn't say anything. Eventually, we make it to the door.

My mom hesitates before knocking.

"Ha!" I think. "So you do get why I..." I can't finish the thought. I never thought I was the kind of person that would actually faint.

My mom takes a deep breath and knocks on the door. I squeeze my eyes shut and... nothing happens. We wait and wait for about 5 minutes, and finally, my mom looks in the window. I look right over her shoulder, and suck in a breath.

The lights are off. Except for one small light. There's a shadow slowly moving, just the way they do in horror movies. By the look of it, it's an old man, and it looks like he's asleep.

I turn around, not wanting to see any more of it, and run to the car.

My mom follows, just walking, but she is speed walking. And her facial expression isn't the reassuring one she usually wears.

My mom opens the door.

"Alright, I think I might've put in the wrong address. Let me try again," she tells me. She pulls out her light gray phone and types in the correct address, and then we start driving. We don't really say anything, though. It's only about a 3 minute drive, but still, when we got there, we're really late.

"It's already 6:00!" my mom exclaims. We hurry out of the car, and I see Lily's face pressing against the front window. She rushes to the door.

"Sorry we're late!" my mom apologizes to Lily's mom, Mrs. Angela, who came to the door with Lily. "I put the wrong address in the GPS."

"Oh, you're fine," assures Mrs. Angela, brushing her long, dark brown hair behind her ear. She always seems like she has everything together.

"Would you like to come in? Although, we should probably get going, I suppose."

"Oh, that sounds fine. I'll just head home to pass out candy! Have fun, girls!"

And with that, we head out to trick-or treat.

"Hi!" I say to Lily, who's wearing her costume with cute earrings that look like little glasses of milk. She looks so much like Mrs. Angela with her long, dark brown hair with small waves that make it ten times as beautiful.

Their skin tone is practically the same, too, with a light brown so light it almost looks golden.

"Hi! I'm so excited! What candy are you hoping for the most?" she responds quickly and with a lot of enthusiasm.

"Hmmm... that's hard. But probably a Twix bar. A big one. I got a huge one last year!" and with that, we start going on and on about previous Halloween experiences and stopping by different houses.

"Everything's fine," I think as Lily tells me a story about when she got a whole box of Swedish Fish in third grade. "That... that house doesn't ever have to be part of my life. Ever, ever, again."

We keep walking along the streets and collecting our candy. When our buckets are almost halfway full, Lily's mom tells us we should turn around soon and walk on the other side of the street.

"How about we go to the street over there, the one to the right, and after we go to those houses, we can turn around?" suggests Lily.

"Alright, sounds good!" I agree. "Want to hear about the time where I got this super sour packet of sour patch kids? Like, they were not supposed to be that sour."

And on go the stories about costumes, candy, houses, people, and soon enough, we aren't even talking about Halloween anymore.

I am so into a story that Lily is telling me about when she climbed up a really tall tree, that I didn't notice it until we were walking straight to it.

"Oh no," I think. "Not again." I stare up at the intimidating house towering over me. I'd never felt so small before.

"Maybe we should turn around," I suggest to Lily shakily.

"You're sure? Let's just get this last house first. Please?" she adds when she notices me hesitating.

I sigh. "Well…"

"I'll take that as a yes!" she decides confidently. Then she pulls me right up to the front door of the house. She knocks loudly.

"Trick-or-treat!" she yells. I look down at my shaking, itchy hands.

"Wow," I think. "Lily sure can persuade." I hold my breath and quickly shut my eyes as the door slowly creaks open.

"Happy Halloween!" says a voice. I open my eyes, blushing.

"Oh," I say, embarrassed. "Thank you." I look up at the man. I had been right.

He is pretty old, but he's not asleep. At least not anymore. His wrinkled face wears a big smile, and he seems really kind.

I look over to Lily, whose eyes are sparkling with delight like she just received a million dollars. I follow her gaze to the candy bucket. It is huge, and it holds probably the most chocolate bars I have ever seen in one place.

"Whoah," I gasp.

"Take two," the man tells us. "Or three or four, if you'd like."

I can't believe it. Up to four giant chocolate bars? Lily and I look up hopefully at Mrs. Angela.

She smiles. "Take however much you want as long as he's fine with it," she says, nodding toward the man. I don't think I ever could've smiled bigger. I take three Twix bars, and one KitKat bar. KitKats are my second favorite. We turn around and start heading to the next house.

"Oh my goodness!" shouts Lily, staring down at her Hershey's bar, Twix bar, Snickers bar, and KiKat bar. "I told you that we should go to that house!"

I grin. "You sure did." And wow, I sure am glad she did. Three whole Twix bars? I still can't believe it.

As we head back, stopping at the last few houses, I realize how glad I am to have a friend like Lily. She always knows what to do. In this case, go to a very creepy house that gives you lots and lots of candy.

And from that day on, I tried to stop being so judgy. I never put a thought into Annie Stacey's clothes with bright pink unicorns that look like they will jump out at you and give you a big hug. I never thought about all the things that Johnny Smith wanted for his birthday, even though his birthday isn't until July.

I never even thought about how rude my friends are and how unfair they were to me. I decided to just be grateful for how everything ended up.

Because, really, being grateful makes my life so much better. And lucky for me, Thanksgiving is next!

About the Author

Nora Sportel is a sixth grade student from Grand Rapids, MI, who loves to write because of the creative and imaginative ideas floating around in her head. Her imagination and curious mind come up with all sorts of ideas and endless "what ifs." When Nora is not writing, she enjoys baking, crafting, reading, playing the piano and playing sports like cross country, basketball and track. She also enjoys fun times with her parents, older sister, younger brother and two adorable cats!

Youth Readers' Choice Winner

To You, From Every Ending Cosmos
Elena Hood

11/08/00

Syon sat on an empty bench as the snow distilled on him. He looked next to him as if someone was supposed to be there by his side, looking at him with starry eyes. Syon couldn't remember her name.

"Those eyes . . . " intoned Syon. "What was her name?" Syon smacked his forehead and tightly closed his eyes.

Tears that looked like stars sprinkled from his face. His mouth quivered and his eyebrows woefully twitched.

The stars twinkled peacefully around the sky as he tried to remember those vague memories with that girl. Syon looked up at the stars, his brown eyes dying forever.

A neon indigo strobe light appeared in the starry gray welkin.

Syon immediately stood up, biting the inside of his lip.

"That color . . . " Syon waited patiently for what was going to happen next. He stood, his thoughts filled with questions and hope.

The star began to luminance incandescently. It got closer, more flamboyant.

Suddenly, it dropped right in front of Syon, blinding his eyes as he staggered backward. "What the . . ?" Syon curiously walked over to the small burnt pile of snow.

A girl with white hair and a long purple dress that was decorated with stars, glitter, and in the front was a stitched symbol that would be described as a celtic love knot layed on the ground. The mystifying girl opened her eyes. The purple and blue colors with faint white clouds and the stellar constellations that settled in her eyes were pulchritudinous. The girl smiled faintly.

Syon gulped. "Who- who are you?"

"I'm Asteria." Asteria sat up from the snow. Those eyes were profound to Syon. It was mysterious, yet sublime.

"What's your name?" asked Asteria softly.

"Syon . . ."

"Syon. A name that is most lovely." Asteria's white hair swirled in the wind, blending in with the snow. "Th-thanks."

Asteria twinkled, laying back down as the snow dropped on her silently.

Reluctantly, Syon decided to lie next to her and watch the twinkling stars and the comforting snow.

"How did you get here?"

"I fell from the stars—I'm a star."

"I mean, why did you come here?"

"No reason, I was bored."

"But you're a star . . ?" Syon looked at Asteria, wonder filling his eyes.

"Yes."

Syon gazed at Andromeda in the dark heavens. He couldn't stop staring, the stars moving ever-so-slightly.

Asteria went above Syon, cupping his head into her hands. Her smile was like the glittering stars including the wonders of the universe.

"How about we stick together?"

Syon quietly gasped. His eyes lit up like ripples of water, broadening.

"With me?" Syon's heart pounded. ". . .Okay. I don't mind." a winter zephyr delicately moved Asteria's hair in the snow. Asteria beamed.

Syon seemed to notice the stars and Andromeda grew brightly.

"You need to go home, the stars say it's late." Asteria's face was full of bliss and mystery. "Yeah . . ."

Asteria looked at Syon in the eyes. She entwined her hand with Syon's.

Everything began to turn a haze, then he felt the warmth of his bed. He shot up, looking at the window in his room open, the moon and stars smiling upon him.

Syon pressed his head against his pillow, thinking about Asteria. Asteria had the essence of the universe and stars on her, the mysteries of this world.

"That girl seemed . . . familiar," reflected Syon. He shut his eyes, everything fading into darkness.

"Syon! Breakfast's ready!"

"Coming," Syon went to the wooden table where pancakes, grits, eggs and bacon appeared on his plate.

"You're happy this morning."

Syon hadn't realized he was smiling.

"Hey, Rosalina." Syon's Daddy kissed Ma on the cheek.

"Oscar, go take that trash out." Ma hissed.

Syon ate the pancakes. This time his Mama made cinnamon pancakes, his favorite. "Whatcha been up to? Didn't see ya last night." Ma looked Syon in the eye, giving Syon the shivers. Syon wanted to tell her, but he merely wanted one thing for himself.

"Walking."

"Come back before nine if you ever go back out again."

"Mhm." Syon quickly ate his breakfast. He couldn't stop thinking about Asteria, how familiar she felt. Syon found it inexplicable.

"Boy, you hidin' something from me? I know that look." Syon looked at his plate. "Mama, I ain't hiding anything."

"Hurry up and eat, K? I gotta go to work." Ma stepped out of her chair and kissed Syon on the forehead. Syon grimaced.

"I love you. Don't wipe off my kiss this time. Deal?" Ma raised her hand in front of Syon's face. Syon chuckled.

They shook hands and Ma went off to work.

Syon stopped smiling. That overwhelming feeling of loneliness winded inside his soul, ruining his day before it started.

Syon grabbed his backpack and walked to school.

English was calming, except the pestiferous kids ruined everything. Mrs. Campbell was once kind, but she's been severely depressed since her son's death.

Algebra was hard. Syon stealthily gave Mr. Georgia a disdainful look. His classmates talked, not knowing Syon existed. Syon raised his hand.

"Question?" Mr. Georgia asked as he turned from the board.

"Restroom." Syon tapped his fingers on the desk. Everyone quieted and listened carefully to Syon's words and movements like he was an animal.

"You interrupted my lesson . . ." he mumbled.

Syon nodded. "Sorry . . ."

"Anyways-"

Syon made his dry voice evanesce from his ears. He looked solemnly at his hand, wishing to go to sleep.

The harsh yellow lighting hit Syon's face.

"Find a partner!" Mr. Rhodes howled into the microphone.

Syon stood at a corner of the gym, watching people find partners except for him. They zoomed past Syon, hugging their best friends while laughing.

Syon began to breathe heavily. "Got a partner?" Mr. Rhodes screamed into the microphone. Syon flinched.

"I wanna work alone . . ." sweat dripped down Syon's face.

Mr. Rhode gave Syon a strange look then walked off.

Syon picked up a volleyball then threw it on a wall back to himself. Tears cascaded from his dead eyes, quickly wiping them hoping no one would see.

He was the only one tossing it onto the wall. Syon's heart raced, hoping for someone, anyone, to tap him on the shoulder and ask him to be his friend.

Syon ran to the bathroom in a different hallway. He silently cried in one of the stalls. Afterwards, he freshened himself up, going back, continuing to be alone.

The bell rang. Syon sprinted home, holding his tears for his pillows.

"Syon!" a girl called. Syon stopped running and looked over. Instantly, he could tell who it was. Asteria walked to Syon who was in front of the school entrance. All of the students' eyes were laid on Asteria and Syon. Whispers rippled through the crowd.

"A-Asteria," Syon's voice quivered. "Please?"

Asteria's visage explained she was puzzled, then she realized.

"Let's go." Asteria grabbed Syon's hand and started running whilst laughing. Syon couldn't help but laugh too.

Syon stole a glance at Asteria's face. Her white eyelashes and hair were lovely. A fluttering feeling set inside his stomach.

"Are we friends?" Syon's eyes looked at Asteria's then back down. "Of course." Asteria tightened her hand. Syon slightly smiled. Syon opened his mouth to speak.

"I don't live with anyone." Asteria said. Syon was confused.

"How did you—?"

"I'm the Titan Greek goddess of the fallen stars. One of my powers is divination." Asteria said casually.

"I believe you." Syon chuckled.

"Maybe we can hangout later to stargaze? . . . I'm sorry." Syon's eyes sagged to the ground. He held the left strap of his backpack with both hands, looking at the right.

"It's okay." Asteria softly said, as she put part of her hair in front of her body. "Actually—"

Asteria put her hand on Syon's shoulder and gazed Syon deep in the swirls of gold in his eyes. Asteria had a firm expression. "You need rest. " Asteria stated.

"All right . . ."

Syon made it home.

"Wassup Syon?" Dad grinned, blinding Syon with glory.

"Hey Dad." Dad patted Syon on the back and put his hand on his shoulder.

"How was school, son?"

"It was good."

"Like everyday? Coo'. " Dad said in a proud tone.

"Ima take a nap." Syon went to his bed and closed his eyes.

Syon saw his hand reaching out for Asteria's. She disappeared as tiny glitter-shaped stars burst into the air in a place that looked like heaven.

Shooting stars scattered the glittery sky and Syon was there, curled in a ball weeping.

Syon burst out of his bed frightened. He took a shower. Afterwards, he wore a baggy black hoodie with cargo pants. Syon touched up his dreads, his hair was fluffy and long to the shoulders. His hair faded to black and brown.

"I'm gonna go out again!" Syon yelled past his parents. He opened the door, not waiting for an answer.

"I'm right here." Asteria stood a few feet away from Syon, her hair elegantly flowing with the wind.

"W-wanna hangout? I'm good now," Syon put his hands in his pockets.

"I do."

With that, they both began to walk to their destination.

Syon and Asteria sat on the ground in a vast yard covered in snow.

Asteria gazed at the stars. Her eyes glinted, showing the reflection of the swirling galaxy in her eyes, making them even more resplendent.

Syon put his hood on, peering at the dark abyss above him. Asteria and Syon sat silent for a moment, appreciating the beauty.

Asteria pointed toward the sky. "Every circle is an essence who formerly dwelled on this earth. Truly prodigious . . ." Asteria seemed deep in thought.

"Hey, Asteria?"

Asteria turned to look at Syon.

"I've never had anyone to be my friend, so . . .thank you. Also, you're the goddess of the fallen stars— I love astronomy, like we were intertwined to be together."

Asteria gazed upon Syon, her hair settling down on her shoulders to the ground. Her lips curled upward, her eyes looking at Syon like he was a precious soul.

He wasn't a match to be friends with someone who was so enchanting to the naked eye.

The way Asteria stared at him made him believe, for one second, that he was important. Butterflies flickered freely in his body.

"I have one request." Asteria put her forehead to Syon's and grabbed his face. "Don't smoke to numb the pain."

"Who told you that?" Syon pulled away from Asteria, tears welling in his eyes.

Syon felt two arms wrap around him. "You have people who care about you. You're not alone, Syon. The stars happen to be evidence of every horrible night you may have, there will still be light waiting for you. I'll try to help."

Syon let the droplets free. He cried for hours, and Asteria was there in that same position, comforting him.

Syon stared at the pack of cigarettes in his drawer. His face darkened as he bit the inside of his lips. Syon looked up at the window, his eyes lifeless.

He picked up the pack of cigarettes he stole from his Mama, throwing it out the window.

11/08/01

"We met a year ago." Asteria declared.

"Remember this spot?" Syon held his scarf.

"Yes. I'm glad I've met you, Syon." Syon sat on the bench he once sat on. When he looked over, he finally had the girl who looked at him with starry eyes.

"When I first met you, I used to have a feeling that I've known you for a long time. I don't know why, it's pretty dumb."

"Now that you've said something, I felt the same way when I met you, too." Asteria grabbed Syon's hand in hers.

"Really?" Syon's voice trembled, looking at his hand weaved with Asteria's. "I bought you a gift," Syon took his backpack off and revealed purple ice skating shoes.

"They look lovely, Syon." Asteria put them on.

"Do they fit?"

"Yes." Syon smiled, putting his on. It was plain black shoes, matching his outfit.

"We should've put them on by the lake." Syon chuckled. "We'll get through the snow together." Syon led the way to the frozen lake.

"I love to skate!" Asteria dashed on the lake and twirled and jumped all over pristinely. "Shall we?" Syon said in a funny voice.

"We shall." Asteria grabbed his hand and they circled each other, then Syon proceeded to pick her up and toss her in the air, back down delicately like a glass vase. Their moves were as smooth and as elegant as the quail.

They danced until their feet ached and told them to stop.

"You were so fluid and confident!" Syon smiled.

"I can say the same." Asteria took her ice skates off and put on her purple heels. "Stargaze?" Syon offered.

"Stargaze."

Asteria and Syon sat in the snow, staring at each other for a brief moment.

"There's something in your hair." Syon pretended to grab something out of Asteria's hair. "Oh- thanks."

Syon smiled and looked at the shining stars, smacking his forehead.

Asteria did not stop staring at him, though. She looked at his charming face and hair, admiring every single detail about him. It saddened her that she felt a way for him, and another. She wheeled her head up towards the cluster of luminaries, two feelings in her heart that contradicted each other.

1/08/01

Syon noticed these last few months Asteria's been acting strangely.

"You've been acting weird these few months. Do you want to go back to . . . your world?" Syon sat on his bed with Asteria.

Asteria remained silent. She avoided Syon's sad eyes.

"I . . . need to go back."

Syon's eyes turned into a brown dot. The sparkle he gained from spending time with Asteria vanished.

"I thought . . ." Syon struggled to say what he was thinking. "What are you . . ?" Syon's voice withered away.

"My parents didn't want me to tell you, but . . ." Asteria's eyes lowered with a slight smile. A tear ran down her cheek. "I couldn't leave you in the dark. I love you." Asteria's body trembled.

Syon took Asteria's chin and stared deep in her eyes. "Asteria, I love you too." Asteria hugged Syon tightly in a pool of tears.

Asteria tightened her grip on Syon's back. "My mother, Phoebe and my father Coeus said they would execute me if I don't come back."

Syon thought of how scared Asteria must've been.

"Despite not seeing me again, I will live on knowing that you've never died to your parents. I'm happy with that."

"But . . .I leave Friday."

"We'll make the most of it."

"I was wondering if I could borrow some money? I'll do anything."

Rosalina smiled. "For that girl? Here you go." Ma handed Syon one-hundred dollars. "Get her something special."

"Thank you."

Syon met up with Asteria at the mall.

"I only have one-hundred, that okay?" Syon said.

Asteria stared at the ground, a mournful smile on her face.

"You don't have to do this."

Syon lended the money to Asteria. Her hand faltered as she tried to grab the dollar.

Finally, she took it and began to look for trinkets. "That's all?"

Asteria nodded.

"I-I don't have anything else planned, but tomorrow I will. Sorry." "Don't be. Much obliged." Asteria said.

Asteria stared at her feet hanging over the mountain ledge.

"The last day." Asteria's hair flew with the wind. "When I set eyes on you behind the sea of stars, would you reminisce back to those days we spent time with each other?" Asteria's curtain bangs gently flew.

"In every ending cosmos and every birthed star, you and I will be reunited."

Syon put a star necklace in his hand and put it in Asteria's.

Asteria stood up and embraced Syon. She let the stars flow freely from her eyes. Her hair of silk spread in the melodic ballad of air and her dress dragged along the rocks.

"I love you." Syon managed to say in tears.

"I love you, too." They looked each other in the eyeballs, not needing to use words to understand what they were feeling. Syon grabbed Asteria's face and put his finger on her chin, still staring at one another. Asteria rested her chin on Syon's shoulder, Asteria's watercolor eyes wrecking with a bombardment of laments and bewails escaping from her eyes.

"I will never forget you . . ." Asteria frailly spoke.

Syon scrunched his eyelids and his mouth quivered. "I promise I won't, even in the next life."

Syon looked at his clock wondering what Asteria is feeling.

It hit midnight, and Syon found himself in a world that was ethereal.

Shooting stars erratically scattered the welkin. Below his feet, he was standing on starry water that reflected the moon. There were also purple asters peeking through the water, flowing with a gentle breeze.

Syon felt a serene wave of calmness wash over him. He let himself slowly fall into the hands of the magical water, the asters surrounding his body.

"I've made your mind come into my abode." Asteria stood above Syon.

Syon immediately got up.

"This is magnificent . . ." Syon smiled. Asteria beamed with her closed eyes.

"I'll miss you, dearly." Asteria gave Syon a gift she'd gotten from the mall.

It was a matching star pendant to the one she was wearing now. It was decorated the same, except Syon's was the moon. Syon clenched it, breathing heavily.

"I'll wear it every single day." Syon put it on.

"Everyone I met will forget about me. My parents said it was best."

Syon's heart crumbled to pieces.

"W-what? Asteria, I-I can't . . !" He was crestfallen from her words.

"I'm sorry." Asteria hugged him. Syon hugged her back, never wanting to forget such a girl.

"In another universe, we shall meet again. Farewell, Syon Jerimoth."

"Goodbye, Asteria." Asteria touched Syon's face, a ripple of water with stars came from her touch. Asteria faded into a glitter of luminaries, leaving Syon curled into a ball, weeping into insanity.

Syon awoke from his doze, the snow still falling on him whilst he sat on an empty bench.

About the Author

Elena Hood is the Write Michigan 2024 Readers' Choice winner in the Youth category.

Youth Published Finalist

Talons and Thrones

Rylan Day

A slender silver creature slithered through the lumbering trees, placing one talon in front of the other hurriedly. Its ears pricked as it stopped short, listening to the slightest sound. Its nostrils flared and its tail lashed as it heaved itself up a mountain slope, every step forced. It let out a shuddered gasp as the rocks crumbled beneath its weight, and it tumbled down the steep terrain. It fell limp beneath the mountain, its body crippled and weak.

Another set of talons clutched the body, piercing it. It raised its head high, and let out a roar of triumph.

"After all these years, you're here, under my talons." The attacking creature let out a twisted laugh. "And now nothing can protect you. Nobody's here for you. You'll die all alone."

The silver creature raised its head weakly and stared at the other snake-like figure. "I may be dying...but you..." It shook the talons away and stood up, though it struggled to maintain balance. "Coldness will take over your heart, until there's no warmth left. You'll become a monster. I will live on, though you will not see me. I'll always guide them to the light. You will hide in the dark, always in pain."

With a shriek of rage, the other creature raked its talons across the silver one's throat. Blood welled up from the wound, and the figure that had been struck jerked once, then collapsed, dead.

"No. It will be you that darkness will swallow. You'll see." The other creature turned, and stalked away, consumed by the shadows.

"Did you hear?" A hushed feminine voice spoke to another dragon.

"What?" A young sienna-colored dragon whispered back.

"Read this." The voice shoved a paper in the sienna dragon's talons. A headline read,

Queen Prism found dead in Mountain Territory!

After General Snare of the Rivertalons went out patrolling, Snare found the queen's body below a mountain. "She was just laying there," Snare said. "There were wounds all over her body, like another dragon had inflicted them on her. It's as if someone ambushed her." Could some cruel dragon have murdered her? Some other clues were...

"Why would anyone want to kill Queen Prism?" The sienna-scaled dragon murmured, taking his gaze away from the newspaper.

"How should I know?" The voice muttered as she curled her tail around her talons. She then folded her wings neatly on her shimmering white scales.

"Frost, do you think that...that someone from our own tribe killed her?" He eyed the white dragon apprehensively as he dropped the paper. She shrugged in response.

"Who knows for sure? After all, her body was found just a few days ago. Don't worry, Bracken. Celestial is a very nice dragon, and she's very controlled. She'll be a wonderful queen. She's nothing like her sister, Gemstone. Between you and me, I think we're lucky that Gemstone isn't around anymore. She was really rude and mean. She would have made a terrible queen." Frost fidgeted with a leaf, which she then let rest on her talons.

"At least Gemstone was older. She knew more things. Celestial may be nice, but she isn't that experienced, or smart," Bracken protested.

"Just accept that Prism and Gemstone are gone. Celestial is the only heir left. She is fit to be queen, and either way, she's going to take the throne."

Frost shot him a sharp look and shook her head. The leaf crunched under her talons. Bracken scowled, but didn't argue.

"I'm sorry. Do you think I shouldn't be queen?" A sleek silver dragon padded up to them, tilting her head. Frost stood up tall, while Bracken's heart lurched.

He'd been caught saying insulting things about Celestial!

"N-no, Your Majesty. I'm sorry. I believe you'd make an excellent queen."

Yet, Bracken felt a prickle on his scales. He couldn't help but feel like danger was nearby. Celestial smiled, and walked away, leaving Bracken embarrassed and scared. Frost nudged him and giggled. "It's not funny, Frost. I-I feel like there's something wrong."

"Well, I don't feel it." Frost rolled her eyes. Bracken's gaze flitted around the area, and turned back to Frost.

"I'm not sure we're safe. I have a feeling." Bracken whispered.

"Come on, Bracken. Let it go. We've lived here most of our lives. We're fine."

Frost reassured him. But Bracken still felt that nagging feeling. "It's almost night, you know. It'd be cool to fly in the dark!" Frost offered.

"But...we aren't necessarily allowed out at night." Bracken lied, trying to find an excuse to stay in the safety of the palace. Frost eyed him, puzzled.

"Did they change that rule?" "Y-yes." Bracken stuttered. Frost hesitated.

"Well, we're going out anyway! Nobody can stop us." Frost spread her wings and lifted into the sky.

"Actually, there's a lot of dragons that can!" Bracken called after her.

He stood, frozen. *I don't want to go. What if there actually is danger?* He sighed, and opened his wings. He raced after Frost, flying behind her. *It's more of a reason to go with her. I can't let her get hurt. She's my friend, and that's not what friends do.* He followed her as she twisted and flew in the sky, and eventually, they arrived at mountain peaks. His heart stopped. *The mountains were where Queen Prism was killed. Surely this place isn't safe?* As they dived down and landed, he turned to Frost. She was staring in awe at the mountains. Bracken's scales prickled again, and his talons trembled.

"Frost," he whispered, "I think we should head back."

"Head back?" Frost echoed in disbelief. "Not me. You can." Bracken stared at her, distraught. *I want to go, but I can't leave her! What should I do?* He glanced at his friend, who was playfully jumping around. I have to protect her. She's unprepared. He concluded. *But what if there isn't anything at all? A part of his mind whispered. Then I'll know that we'll be okay.* After around an hour, he and Frost curled up on the mountain, and the soothing sounds of night relaxed him. He looked over at Frost to make sure she was alright, but she was in a deep sleep. He closed his eyes, comforted, and fell asleep.

A shriek startled Bracken awake. He glanced up at the sky. It was as black as night could be. He frowned. It was still very late. But his talons itched and his scales pricked uncomfortably. He could sense something was wrong.

Bracken looked over at Frost--or, where Frost was supposed to be.

His legs faltered and his eyes were wide with panic. "Frost!" He called out. He scanned the clearing and with horror, saw a trail of blood. He paused. *If I follow it, I could die. It's probably a trap. But that doesn't matter,* he added, and raced across the trail. *I can't let her die.* He followed the trail into a wooded area, and finally reached the end of the path. Bracken's stomach dropped as he saw Frost, laying unmoving on the ground. Her scales were glistening, but they weren't white anymore. They were splotched with blood. Bracken hurried over to her, but was aware of peering eyes watching him. He gasped as he saw a deep gash in Frost's neck, and many scratches alongside her flank. Bile rose in his throat.

"Show yourself!" He spat. "If you dared to attack my friend, you'll have to get through me!" Whatever--or whoever it was--let out a twisted laugh.

"I love your enthusiasm, but I'm afraid no one has survived me. Not even poor Prism..." The voice shook with triumph.

Bracken felt as if stones were in his belly. *This is who killed Prism.* He realized he should not have threatened this dragon. *If this is really who they say they are, then who I'm dealing with is more dangerous than I thought...*

He stared at Frost desperately. *Please wake up. I don't want to die here, alone.*

"I'm in a good mood tonight, so I'll give you a chance, little dragon."

The voice growled. "Take your friend and run. Get out of here. Accept that Prism is dead, and side with Celestial. Or you can die." Bracken hesitated. He whipped around to look at Frost. She was breathing, but she was unconscious and the wound in her neck looked deep. *This is the only way.* He thought solemnly.

"Alright, I'll go. But please," Bracken's voice was hoarse. "Please don't hurt her again."

The dragon snorted, but growled in agreement. "Just get out of here and be loyal to your new queen." Bracken lifted Frost onto his back, and with a pang of sorrow, realized how light she was.

She's losing blood. I have to get her back. He opened his wings, and aired into the sky. He kept on flying, even though his wings were sore, until he saw a palace. He made sure Frost was balanced on his back before he dived down into the stone building. As he plummeted down, he noticed a dragon behind him. The stones in his stomach dropped further. Is that dragon following us? I thought it said it'd leave us alone. He shook his head.

It's probably not the same dragon. He touched red carpet and noticed the chandeliers above him.

Bracken let out a sigh of relief. I'm in the palace. He glanced at Frost, who had slid off his back and was now on the ground next to him.

"Bracken!" A dragon screamed. "What happened to you?"

Bracken looked up and recognized Pebble, one of Prism's chefs. She was as young as him and Frost, but she knew how to cook well. She was staring with wide eyes at Bracken's claws, which were covered in Frost's blood.

"I'll explain later. Please get one of the healers," he pleaded. Pebble nodded, and dashed away in the direction of the healer's hut. Bracken pressed against the wound in Frost's neck, hoping to stop the bleeding before it progressed. He paused as he heard thundering steps coming racing towards him. Moments later, a blue and white dragon appeared, holding bandages. Bracken let out a sigh of relief.

"Good idea, Bracken," the blue dragon nodded as he spotted Bracken's talons. "But use this instead. It's more effective and will help her regain strength." He pushed the bandage to him.

Bracken picked it up and carefully laid it on Frost's gash. The bandage was long enough to cover the whole wound. Pebble was standing beside the healer, looking nervously at Bracken.

"Can I do anything to help?" She asked. The blue dragon shook his head. "Leave it to me."

More talon steps followed, and General Snare appeared. Bracken stared, surprised.

"Is she alright?" His gruff voice echoed off the halls. Bracken noticed that Snare was peering at him. Snare's yellow eyes glinted maliciously, seeming to bore into Bracken's soul. Bracken's breath caught in his throat. Snare jerked his head to Frost with narrowed eyes. The general's tongue flicked in and out of his mouth.

Bracken caught sight of Snare flexing his claws, and was aware that the wound on Frost's neck had been inflicted by a big, burly dragon with long talons.

"Make sure she'll be alright," Bracken stared at the healer and nodded to Frost. I have to report this to Celestial. But a prickle in his scales told him he should run away. No. I have to do this. He raced down the hallway, and turned to the Throne Room. He looked back to make sure no one had followed him.

He saw Celestial sitting on her throne with her head raised high.

"Bracken," her voice was cool and unfriendly, unlike her normal soft sound. "I was expecting you."

Bracken stared in confusion at her. The prickle got stronger and his legs trembled. There was a rumbling sound, and after a few seconds, Snare appeared behind him. The sandy-colored dragon let out a laugh that boomed through the walls.

"You should have listened to Snare," Celestial's gaze sharpened and she curled her talons. "I've had my doubts for a while, but now I'm sure. You're just like my mother. Always assuming. I'm actually quite smart. Smarter than I'd let you believe." She grinned. "Why do you think Gemstone went missing, and Prism suddenly died?"

Bracken felt as if he were numb. The world collapsed around him. "You killed them." he breathed. Celestial smirked.

"Snare did the honors of killing Gemstone and Prism and injuring your little friend. But it was me who came up with the plan. Smart, huh?" She eyed the general, who bared his teeth at Bracken. "And now, we must kill you."

"You killed them!" Outrage filled Bracken's retort. "And you hurt Frost!"

"And who do you think you'll tell before you die?" Snare snarled. Bracken realized that he was surrounded by two larger and stronger dragons. He couldn't escape without being injured, at the least. He hesitated as the dragons circled him, then bolted out of the Throne Room. Celestial and Snare were on his tail.

Bracken raced fearfully through the palace, hoping to lose them. He swiveled around every turn, but everytime he looked back, they were still chasing him.

Eventually, Bracken found himself pressed against a wall.

"Well, well. Would you look at the scared little dragonet?" Snare sneered.

Celestial padded up to Bracken and swifty sliced him across the nose.

He winced as pain stung him.

"It's time you forgot any of this happened." Snare raised his talons, but before he could strike, Bracken a familiar white-scaled dragon darted in front of Snare and tripped the general. Snare fell back and toppled over Celestial. Frost glared at them, and moments later, guards with spears piled in. Frost pointed with a talon outstretched to Celestial and Snare.

"They're the ones you want."

"Get off me!" Celestial barked as guards tugged her out from under Snare.

"Don't touch me!" The guards ignored her, and in stone cold silence, cuffed Snare and Celestial.

"Get these off me!" Celestial demanded. "I am your queen. You listen to me!"

"You're not the queen anymore." Frost stood her ground, facing Celestial with blazing icy eyes. "You killed Prism and Gemstone and attacked me and Bracken. What kind of queen would do that?" She nodded towards the guards.

"When I regained consciousness, I told the guards and Blueberry--" She dipped her head to the blue and white healer--"what happened and that it was Snare who attacked me."

Celestial growled, but said nothing. Snare bellowed as guards tied up his snout, lashing out at the armored dragons.

"We've caught you." Bracken panted, exhausted from running. "You brought this on yourself, you know."

Snare growled, and Celestial stared at him with cold eyes.

Frost raised her head and faced the guards. "Tell everyone there will be a meeting in the auditorium. Gather every dragon inside this palace. Now." The guards nodded and rushed away, while Frost turned her gaze to Celestial and Snare.

"Princess Celestial and General Snare." Frost began, her tail slithering on the ground. "You are charged with murder, and therefore will be banished forever. See it as a chance. We could easily kill you both now, but we're giving you an opportunity to live. After the meeting is held, you two will flee from this place forever. If we catch sight of you, know that guards will be all over you. And next time, they will not show mercy." Frost padded away, leaving the chained dragons on the stony floor.

"Should they have guards?" Bracken asked, following Frost.

"No. Come on. Let's go tell everyone the truth." They walked beside each other, and Bracken realized how strong Frost was now.

"Do you feel okay?" Bracken asked, concerned. Frost smiled. "I've never felt better." Bracken yawned and stretched his wings. It had almost been a year since Celestial and Snare were banished. Every dragon was furious with the former queen and general, and they hadn't caught sight of the outcasts yet. But Bracken knew they were out there somewhere, waiting for another couple of mindless dragonets. He hadn't grown that much older, but he was wiser now. He was more careful, and learned to listen to the prickly feeling. Frost was more mature, too. The gash in her neck had healed, but left a massive scar. The other scratches had simply disappeared after they healed. Bracken glanced over at Frost. She was resting beside him, fast asleep.

After the meeting where Frost revealed Celestial and Snare's crimes, every dragon held a vote where they decided on the new queen. Almost everyone had chosen Frost. Frost seemed like the logical choice. She was clever and fit enough to take the throne. He felt proud that his friend was respected and at a higher rank, but missed the days when they hung out. She was busy now, but at least she had some time for him. He looked at the palace, and puffed out his chest as he watched parents teaching their children, and guards looking after everyone. Bracken knew that while everyone was still cautious, everyone felt more peace than they had in years. Bracken snuggled up closer to Frost, closed his eyes, and fell asleep, comforted by his friend.

The end

About the Author

Rylan Day is an 11-year-old writer who has a fascination with animals. She owns a very cute chinchilla named Violet. Rylan is inspired by Erin Hunter's Warriors series and Tui Sutherland's Wings of Fire series. She loves to draw and is a music enthusiast. Rylan has amazing friends and loves to hang out with them.

Youth Published Finalist

The Boy and the Dove: A Short Story
Emma Krueger

Leo was sitting on the windowsill, staring out at the blank landscape. Hills of dirt and sand blocked half the view, and the dust particles swarmed around them like early morning fog. He wiped his brow, settling a knee over the other.

Nothing's the same. Not since dad- No. Leo shut his eyes tightly, pushing away the memory. *It's all mom's fault. I just- I can't believe it.* He opened his eyes, glowering at the ground.

"Mom, you said it would stop," Leo called without glancing behind him. There was a sigh, and Leo's mom appeared, in her arms two overflowing boxes.

She set them down beside her son, touching his shoulder lightly.

"I said that the Mayor will do what she can."

Leo flinched, looking up. "You know it won't get better! Just look!" He pointed out the window. Leo's mom looked out the window, her face darkening.

She didn't blink, breathing in deeply. Leo just watched her, eyes glassy. Without a word, the mother turned away from her son.

"It will get better. Start unpacking in the meantime." Leo gave the boxes a glare, angrily clenching his fists. "It won't, and you know it." Leo's voice was soft, nothing more than a whisper, but his mom must have heard it.

She tensed.

1 MONTH LATER

Leo laid in his bed, thinking. He coughed, waving his hand. A whole month had passed, leaving him more restless than ever, and the dust had gotten worse.

It hadn't rained in days, and a fire had broken out in Leo's own backyard.

A footstep brought Leo from his thoughts. He looked up, narrowing his eyes when he spotted his mother's slender frame.

"Unless you've saved the world, you'd better leave." Leo felt a pang of guilt as his mom flinched, but continued. "This is all your fault. Making us move."

"I was doing the best for you—"

"No, you weren't!"

"At school you can find new friends—"

"I can't even go OUTSIDE!" Leo was nearly screaming now, his hands curled into fists. His mom bit her lip, eyes filling with unshed tears. "Your Father wanted this. This was his house."

Leo closed his eyes. "Well, now he's gone." As soon as the words left his mouth, Leo regretted it.

The door closed silently, and a muffled sob broke the silence. Leo glanced at the window, the curtains half-drawn. It was dark.

Maybe sleep would wash away the pain.

Yes, thought Leo, maybe it will.

At first there was silence and a smothering blackness.

Then there was a tapping.

Leo shot up like a rocket, heart pounding. He turned his head, eyes flickering from side to side as he searched for the source of the noise.

tap

tap

tap

Leo widened his eyes, sweeping his gaze across his room. A flicker of white caught his attention. *tap*

tap

tap

Slowly creeping towards the noise, Leo blanched as he stared out the window.

A dove sat on the windowsill.

A dove.

Leo fumbled with the window latch, pulling open the rusted slider. A blast of gritty wind slapped his face, and he winced. He looked down at the dove, willing it to come inside.

The dove dipped its head, displaying a single black mark. In the shape of a star.

It waddled inside, looking up at Leo curiously. Leo quickly shut the window, blinking fast. "There, there," Leo wondered how to handle the bird.

The dove just stared at Leo, and something in its gaze triggered him.

Leo leaned down beside the dove, stroking its back. It cooed, fluffing its feathers. This was clearly what it wanted.

But why?

Leo walked over to his bed, glancing back at the bird.

It flew to him, nuzzling his sweater.

At that moment, Leo spotted a ring of red.

Plastic, restricting the little dove's movement.

A flash of resent made Leo narrow his eyes, anger clear in his face.

The dove blinked. It lowered itself to the blanket, shivering. Leo's resent vanished.

The dove did not want anger. It wanted peace.

Leo stared into the bird's milky eyes, carefully undoing the plastic. It fell off, and the dove hopped happily.

Leo smiled, despite himself.

Leo spent the night staring into that dove's eyes.

Until he drifted off, hand still gingerly stroking the silver-white bird's feathers.

*Leo was back at his old house. The halls.

That mirror.

The desk.

It was Leo's father's office.

Leo widened his eyes, scanning the moonlit room.

In the dark corner, a girl sat, her skin a pure white. A shard of fear stabbed Leo in the chest when he saw it.

The star.

On the girl's neck.

It glowed unnaturally, pulsing coldly.

"Let go." The girl had spoken. She was looking at Leo,

and something in her gaze was familiar. Her iris was black. The dove.

Leo backed away, questions swirling in his head.

"Let go of what?"

"The anger." The girl shifted, lifting her head. "Let it go."

Leo paused.

He opened his palm, looking straight ahead.

"How?"

The girl blinked at him, serenely. "You already did."

Glancing at the open window, the girl rose. The black star on her neck shone. "Now let go of the dove."*

...

Leo awoke, feeling at his side.

The dove was gone.

A single feather lay on the bed.

Leo lowered his head, weeping silent tears. And yet, joy swept him. Leo stood, walking over to the window.

The dove was free.

The anger was gone.
And the sky was-- blue.

About the Author

Emma Krueger has been telling stories since she could speak, and when not speaking, she is singing. Dedicated to finishing her novel, *The Last King*, by the end of the year, she balances her spare time with songwriting, poetry, sketching, and animation. Emma enjoys curling up on the couch with a good book and her two dogs.

Youth Published Finalist

The Seven Principles
Hunter Miller

Chapter One

AARON

ONE DAY, I'm awake, breaking the rules again. The next, I'm silent, and I do not break anything. The only thing that naturally breaks is the sun after dawn.

Sometimes, I swear the clouds are black, preventing the moon from coming alive at night.

I shove out of bed, leaving my sheets in complete disarray. Life is too short to care about making the bed, especially when you're me.

Being a Fowler sucks. We're known for our reputation, and I've already fulfilled the world's expectations of me at age sixteen.

You know what also sucks? Juvie. Being arrested for multiple kinds of theft, including hijacking cars and swiping credit cards from a man's back pocket.

And now it's Christmas. Lonely, boring Christmas. The day I won't find any presents under my Christmas tree–scratch that, I don't even have a Christmas tree.

I walk into my kitchen and over to the sink where I fill up a glass of water.

I take a sip, almost swallowing before looking at my orange reflection in the water. *Orange?*

I immediately spit the rusty tap water into the sink, dumping the rest of my cup down the drain.

I really need to get a water filter.

I lean against the counter and blink a few times, opening my eyes, but I don't see anything new. Only the blank, pictureless walls of my sister's house and the gloomy light emerging from behind closed curtains—in a nutshell, nothing interesting. Nothing is ever interesting when you're a Fowler, and that's why we resort to crime. We resort to crime because we already have a target on our backs, so there's no point in trying to be upstanding citizens.

I grab my fairly lightweight backpack, which is home to nothing besides my school essentials and overdue homework, and head out the door, making sure to ignore the overgrown bushes and weeds consuming the small house.

As I make my way to school, I watch the other kids laugh and push their friends around.

Friends, as in the things I've never had.

They all stop to gawk at me as I pass. Their expressions speak louder than words ever could.

A Fowler? My God, run while you still can.

And they do exactly that.

I don't know what my mom was thinking when she chose this neighborhood full of unaccepting people. It's a strange question I may never receive an answer to. It's not like my mom would even care to talk to me in the first place. If she ever came home, she'd probably rather talk to my twin sister, Tarryn.

Tarryn is the only thing left in this family that resembles innocence, though we both know that's only what our mother thinks. I see the way Tarryn acts around the people she calls friends. I see the way she steals their spare change and the items in their pockets. I see the way she slips into the shadows at night, lost in claustrophobic alleys and running down twisted streets.

But me? Everyone sees me as the only thing I don't want to be; a criminal. I have no desire to follow in Tarryn's footsteps.

I realize that schools are closed on this day called Christmas, but I refuse to return to the place where I am not wanted. The only place I'm supposed to belong, but I don't. I'm still an outsider inside my home.

Instead, I climb up to my refuge on the school's front steps and take a seat.

I watch people make uneven snow angels and snowmen and throw snowballs at each other. *Snow. So much snow.*

No one cares when they look up to see an unwanted sixteen-year-old boy sitting atop the steps of a closed school.

"Shouldn't you be celebrating with your family?"

I jump, startled by the sudden appearance of a girl to my left.

"Go away!" I snap.

Wait, what? She's talking to me?

"How about no?" She smiles, leaning closer to me, setting her head in her hand. "My family doesn't want me," I mutter in response, folding my arms to my chest. She sticks her tongue out at the sky, catching a snowflake and gulping it down as if I'm not even there.

"Why are you doing that?" I ask, scrunch up my face.

"It's entertaining. Look! Catch one!" She points to one falling toward me.

I eye her before sticking my tongue out, simultaneously rolling my eyes. I let it melt in my mouth before swallowing. "There, happy?"

"Not until you are," she says, mimicking my look of disgust. It almost makes me laugh.

"You're horrible at feigning disgust."

"Anything to make a friend smile," she replies with a wide grin. I wouldn't consider us friends, but I get the general idea.

"So, what are you planning on doing for Christmas?" I ask, my eyes suddenly downcast at the subject.

"We don't celebrate Christmas," she replies.

"What? That's crazy!" I exclaim.

Then again, I don't either.

"I follow a different faith," she explains, averting her eyes to the snow to avoid my gaze.

"Oh, I didn't realize."

"It's fine," she says with a wide smile. "My name is Adara. What's yours?"

"Aaron," I reply, feeling my face when my mouth contorts into a smile against my will.

"Nice to meet you, Aaron," she replies.

Something vibrates, and then Adara pulls a phone out of her pocket.

"Not her again..." She contemplates for a moment before finally sweeping a thumb across the screen and holding her phone up to her ear.

I don't ask.

"Hello?" She says through gritted teeth.

I tilt my head back, watching snowflakes of every shape and size fall through the bright blue sky.

"Delaney, how many more times am I going to tell you 'no'? What part of that word do you not understand?" Adara shouts. "I don't want to come to your stupid party. Please leave me alone." And with that, she hangs up with a long, frustrated sigh. "Sorry, Aaron."

"It's fine. If you don't mind me asking, who was that?" I ask.

"Her name is Delaney. We went to high school together. She keeps inviting me to her Christmas party and she's not taking no for an answer," Adara replies. "Excuse me? My Christmas party is not stupid!" A blonde-haired girl with hypnotic brown eyes yells. She's standing at the bottom of the staircase, squinting up at us.

Her long hair is braided over her shoulder. She's wearing a violet turtleneck sweater and plaid pajama pants that don't match.

"Are you stalking me?" Adara says, pointing an accusatory finger at the girl. "No, I just happen to be getting takeout," she gestures to the paper bags in her hands.

"Can you not cook?" Adara smirks.

"I can, I just don't have time."

"I doubt that," Adara laughs.

"Girls!" I mediate. "Why are you fighting?"

They simultaneously point fingers at each other, speaking at the same time.

"She thinks my Christmas party is dumb!"

"I have nothing to celebrate!"

I sigh, massaging my forehead with my palm. "We don't have to fight about this–"

"Yes, we do!" They shout in unison.

"Let's just sort out our differences and be at peace. There is an alternative," I say, a little surprised that they didn't cut me off.

"I don't care about your stupid alterna–wait, alternative?" Delaney knits her brows together, cocking her head. "Well, go on!" She says impatiently.

"There's a seven-day celebration of culture and traditional values starting tomorrow called Kwanzaa," I explain.

"*Ohhhh*, I've heard about that," Delaney nods. "But isn't that just for African Americans?"

"And what about the accepted religions?" Adara adds.

"No, Kwanzaa is for everyone, no matter what race or religion," I say.

"Can we still celebrate Christmas if we celebrate Kwanzaa?" Delaney says, using her hands to speak.

"If you want to. Kwanzaa is a very open and welcoming holiday," I tell them. "Then we're in. It starts tomorrow, right? You guys can come to my house then," Delaney declares.

"Oh, no way–I just found a solution for you guys. I wasn't implying anything about me coming–"

"Come on, Aaron, you don't have anyone else to celebrate with, right?" Adara asks me, knocking me in the arm with her own.

"Well, no, but–"

"Then it's official, you are coming to my house tomorrow," Delaney proclaims.

"Girl, I barely know you. I'm not sure if I feel safe coming to your house yet," I say drily like that should have been obvious.

"Well then," Delaney dramatically begins, searching her pockets for a small pad of paper and a pen. She scribbles something down, climbing the steps to hand it to me. "Here's my number in case you change your mind."

I don't think I will, but I take it anyway, just to be polite. I manage a smile. "Sure. Thanks," I say, with unintentional dullness.

She frowns. "Sure. Thanks," she mocks. "You're welcome, I guess."

"Sorry," I say, genuine.

She just descends the stairs, her back to me and her hands in her pockets. She pivots when she reaches the bottom. "My friends are probably wondering where I am by now. I have to go. See you," she says unenthusiastically. She looks slightly dismal as she drags herself away, kicking the snow from her path.

"Sorry about her. She's bipolar, so don't be surprised if she acts energetic one minute and depressed the next," Adara tells me.

"That's terrible," I say.

"Yeah, it is," Adara agrees. She stands up, squinting at a building in the distance. "Hey, what do you say we go get some coffee?" She offers.

"Sorry, I can't. I have until New Year's to save up for high school. I can't spend my money on frivolous things," I say, rising beside her. I look at her for a moment and she looks at me.

"Don't worry about it. I'll cover yours."

"What? Really? You would do that for me, a total stranger?" "Like I said, anything for a friend."

"I like you," I say. "You seem like a real friend." "Um...thanks?"

"Crap, sorry, I'm just not used to meeting real friends. Everyone I've ever befriended has either dumped me for my twin sister Tarryn or thrown me under the bus."

"I'm sorry that happened to you. We're going to be good friends, I promise. Now come on, let's go get some coffee." She grabs my hand, pulls me down the steps. And for the first time ever, I think this is my chance to finally be happy.

Chapter Two

DELANEY

I SLIDE DOWN to the wooden floor against my door, sobbing into my knees. I feel like screaming and I don't know why.

I pound my fists into my pillow, stuff my face into it and scream.

Stronger. Louder. Faster.

I stop when I hear a knock on my door.

"Delaney, you've been in there for a while. Are you okay?" It's Sierra.

In an attempt to hush my ragged breath, I only make it worse. It's like my entire body is lifting instead of just my chest. I'm shaking and I'm freezing and I'm *tired, tired, tired.*

"I'm coming in," she forewarns me, but it won't work. My door is locked.

"Delaney," Sierra begins, cautious. "Open the door."

"No!" I scream. The music is so loud that it drowns it out. But I know Sierra hears me. She always has. She hears me when I cannot speak. When I'm at my lowest | low and my highest high. When I feel like giving up, she hears me.

"Delaney, open your door or I'll break it down."

"Okay, okay," I wipe my nose on my bare arm. "Coming."

I open the door, the flashing lights almost blinding me.

"You've been sitting in the dark?" She says, pauses. "And crying."

"No," I lie. "I put red makeup under my eyes."

"Don't you dare start that with me. You know it won't work."

"I know," I give in. "It just hurts less when I don't admit it."

"Oh, come here," she says, wrapping her arms around me. "You know you can come to me if you're feeling down. I'm always here for you."

"I didn't want to burden you with my problems when you were having a good time. You were really enjoying the party. It's Christmas. We're supposed to be happy and thankful and excited. Not–whatever this is."

"I don't care if it's Christmas or Hanukkah or my birthday or even if I'm on my deathbed. I want to know how you feel. Honesty is one of the biggest parts of friendship. I don't want you to keep anything from me or vice versa. Please just come to me next time, okay?"

"Okay," I agree.

I don't know if I will follow these 'ground rules', but I try to sound confident. I think it worked because she's smiling. I smile too.

"Come on," Sierra grabs my hand. "Let's go enjoy your party."

I FISH AROUND for the ringing phone in my bag, eager to see who it is. I grab ahold of it and hoist it out, staring at the screen. Unknown number. I answer it in hopes of it being Aaron.

"Hello?"

"Hi," I say nervously, biting at a hang nail on my index finger.

"Delaney, hey," Aaron says. So it is him. "I've changed my mind. I'm getting around to come to your house now. We'll be there in a few."

"We?" I ask. "Who's with you?"

"Adara. She knows where you live. I can't get there without her."

"Oh, okay," I grit my teeth slightly. "That's fine."

"Okay! We're heading out the door now. See you in a few. Bye."

"See you," I reply. I'm the first to hang up. I set my phone face down on the counter, yelling, "YES!" and throwing my hands in the air.

"Well, something good must've happened," Sierra says, walking into the kitchen and leaning on the counter, a cup of coffee in her hand.

"Yep!" I squeal. "We're having a second, seven-day-long Christmas."

"Third for me. Geez, so I'm adding another Christmas to my December calendar? First I had Hanukkah, then Christmas, and now an anonymous holiday? That's great."

"It's called Kwanzaa," I tell her.

"Isn't that–"

"All religions and races are accepted," I quickly explain.

"Okay then."

Two beats. Three.

I practically dance to the door, but I immediately stop when a sharp, aching pain jolts through my legs. I had already done enough dancing in the past twenty-four hours. It's the unfortunate result of having a party.

I twist the doorknob, coaxing it open until I meet Aaron's dazzling brown eyes, see his warm, tan skin glowing in the sunlight–oh, yeah, Adara is here too. Kind of forgot about her for a second.

I shake my head, snapping myself out of it. "Hi," I manage.

"Hey!" Aaron grins. "I brought the *Kinara.*"

"The what?" I blink.

"It's Swahili for candle holder. There are seven candles for the seven nights," Aaron beams. I can tell he hasn't celebrated Kwanzaa in years.

"Cool," I nod.

Adara places a crockpot on the counter, plugging it in. "We brought corn, mashed potatoes, honey ham, mac n' cheese, etcetera. I hope you're hungry," Aaron winks.

I giggle. "Starving."

After sitting down with our steaming plates of–well, there's so many foods that I can't even put a name to them all–Sierra gives us our appetizer of...comedy. She does that.

"Why didn't the skeleton go to the party?" She asks, a smug grin on her face as she leans in on the table with her elbows.

"Why?" Adara inquires, a quarter of her plateful already gone.

"Because he had no body to go with," Sierra howls at her own joke.

Aaron cracks a grin, but he's preoccupied with peeking at me in his peripheral vision.

I think my cheeks are sweating? Well, that's new.

I avoid his gaze, watching the candlelight flicker on the black, middle candle on the *Kinara.* Aaron clears his throat. "Tonight's principle is Umoja, or, in English, unity. During these six days and seven nights, we may recite poems written by African Americans if we so choose. We may also exchange gifts on the last day, New Years. Each night has a different principle. The most important thing about Kwanzaa is having fun. For the most part, there are no rules on how Kwanzaa is celebrated. However, there are traditions. Typically, Keramu, the feast, is on the sixth day, though I personally choose to have the feast on the first day." After Aaron finishes his speech, I take their plates and set them in the sink.

Turning to the dancing flame, I extinguish the fire with my breath, watching the smoke rise through the air. Aaron and Adara help me clean up, rinsing their plates and loading the dishwasher. I gratefully smile at them, but then I look back at Sierra with the I'm so done with you look. She gives me puppy eyes in return.

Aaron closes his hand around mine, smiling that Fowler smile at me. My cheeks burn, like someone had just cranked the knobs on a stove. It takes me a moment to smile back. He lets go when I do.

I shove my hand in my pocket but still feel it tingling from his touch.

"We should get going," Aaron says. "It's getting late."

"You're right," Adara nods.

"Bye, Delaney. See you tomorrow?" He says it like a question.

"Yeah," I say, half grinning and staring at my feet. I meet his eyes. "Tomorrow."

"Bye," he says for the final time and retreats out of the door, waving behind him.

As I collapse into my bed, I shake off my slippers and pull the covers tight, wrapping myself like a burrito. Unity, I think. Tonight was the night of unity, and when I drift into a world of imagination, I feel as though the world has united me with every feeling, every touch. The world has united us.

About the Author

Hunter Miller is a growing author, performer of every kind, and pet lover. Her potential career as an author, ballerina, aerial artist, singer, and voice actress means everything to her. You can find her designing book covers, cuddling with her chihuahua-mix, sharing coffees with her older sister, and putting all of her energy into writing her debut novel, *Anonymous*.

About Write Michigan

The Write Michigan Short Story Contest began in 2012 as a dream. Kent District Library Director Lance Werner envisioned libraries and publishers working together to highlight the efforts of Michigan writers via an independently published book. What better way to interest readers and writers than a writing contest? Writers could create a short story; readers could read those short stories. Nearly 600 writers from all over the state entered the inaugural contest. Author Wade Rouse contributed the foreword to the first anthology.

For the twelfth annual contest, founding partners KDL and Schuler Books along with partners Capital Area District Library, Canton Public Library and Michigan Learning Channel received submissions from 333 zip codes across the state of Michigan. With almost 1,200 entries, the contest had 124 reviewers to narrow the field to ten semi-finalists in each category. Eight judges determined the Judges' Choice and Runner-Up winners, while more than 2,000 public votes were cast to determine the Readers' Choice winners in each category. Cash prizes amounting to $3,000 were distributed to the winners.

With such overwhelming success, the Write Michigan Contest has established itself as a premier writing contest in the Mitten State. Libraries and bookstores share the goal of fueling interest in libraries, writing and reading. The Write Michigan Short Story Contest is an integral part of that goal.

2024 Judges

CAITLIN HORROCKS

Caitlin Horrocks is author of the story collections *Life Among the Terranauts* and *This is Not Your City,* both *New York Times* Book Review Editor's Choice titles. Her novel *The Vexations* was named one of the 10 best books of 2019 by t*he Wall Street Journal.* Her stories and essays appear in *The New Yorker, The Best American Short Stories, The PEN/O. Henry Prize Stories, The Pushcart Prize, The Paris Review* and elsewhere. She lives with her family in Grand Rapids, Michigan, where she teaches at Grand Valley State University.

JANYRE TROMP

Janyre Tromp is a veteran book editor by day and writer of mid-20th century historical novels with a healthy dose of intrigue and myth by night. She's the award-winning and bestselling author of *Shadows in the Mind's Eye* and co-author of both O *Little Town* and *It's a Wonderful Christmas.* And that all happens from her unfinished basement when she's not hanging out with her family, two troublesome cats, and slightly eccentric Shetland Sheepdog.

You can find her on social media and her website: **JanyreTromp.com**

JAY WHISTLER

Jay Whistler (she/her) holds an MFA in Writing for Children and Young Adults from the Vermont College of Fine Arts. She is an author, freelance editor, former acquisitions reader for three literary agencies, an editor for an online short story anthology and a print anthology, and has been a judge for numerous writing contests. She regularly gives presentations on the craft of writing at local, national and international writing and publishing conferences. Her two current titles, *The Ghostly Tales of San Antonio* and *The Ghostly Tales of Put-In-Bay,* are nonfiction historical middle-grade books, both using ghost stories to tell history.

You can learn more about her at: **JayWhistler.com**

JODI MCKAY

Jodi lives in Grosse Pointe, Michigan with her husband and son. She is the author of two picture books, *Where Are the Words?* and *Pencil's Perfect Picture,* both published by Albert Whitman & Co. Jodi is the Co-Regional advisor for the Michigan chapter of the Society of Children's Book Writers and Illustrators and is represented by Linda Epstein of the Emerald City Literary Agency.

You can learn more about her at: **JodiMcKayBooks.com**

JOEL ARMSTRONG

Joel Armstrong is a speculative fiction writer whose stories have appeared in *Asimov's Science Fiction, Analog Science Fiction* & Fact, Daily Science Fiction and NewMyths.com. He has also published poetry and literary criticism in *SUFI, Clues: A Journal of Detection,* and *The Hemingway Review.* By day, he is a content editor and product developer for an indie book publisher based in West Michigan. In his free time, he likes to garden vegetables, enjoy Michigan's beaches and take long walks. He lives in the Boston Square neighborhood of Grand Rapids with his doulatog wife and their two naughty cats.

MIKE SALISBURY

Mike Salisbury's fiction has appeared in *Black Warrior Review, Midwestern Gothic,* and *Crab Orchard Review,* among others. Mike is a graduate of the MFA program at Pacific University. He is the co-creator of the graphic novel The Quarry, published fall 2023 by Scout Comics. As a literary agent at Yates & Yates, he has worked with several *New York Times* bestselling authors, including Jen Hatmaker, Jon Acuff, Latasha Morrison and John Mark Comer. He lives with his wife and daughters along Michigan's West Coast.

You can learn more about publishing, writing and working with Mike at **Authorcoaching.com.** Connect with Mike on Instagram and LinkedIn.

TERRI DEBOER

After more than 30 years as a broadcast meteorologist, Terri DeBoer is "changing seasons" and joining the retirement specialists at Jacobs Financial Services as Director of Communications. As a published author, Terri has recently released her third book, *Encore Season: Making the Rest of Your Life...the Best of Your Life.*

TRINITY MCFADDEN

Trinity McFadden has been a literary agent with The Bindery since 2020, where she represents a diverse group of authors writing compelling practical and narrative nonfiction, poetry, fiction and children's literature. Her focus is especially on seeking to promote under-represented voices with growing platforms. Before The Bindery, she worked in traditional publishing for more than 12 years in editorial and public relations roles at various companies, including HarperCollins Christian and Baker Publishing Group. Trinity earned a bachelor's degree in philosophy and recently finished her master's degree in business administration. She lives in Grand Rapids, Michigan, with her husband and daughter.

More information on The Bindery can be found at: **TheBinderyAgency.com**

Acknowledgments

For the past twelve years, the Write Michigan Short Story Contest has helped authors share their stories with the world. This has been made possible, first and foremost, by authors of all ages who put pen and pixels to paper and screen to tell stories of love, life, adventure, pain, healing and more. This year, nearly 1,200 entries were received from across Michigan, vying for a chance to be featured in this anthology, and we applaud each author for sharing their story.

More than 120 volunteers reviewed the entries this year, not only scoring the entries but also providing authors with helpful feedback. The review process determined finalists which were advanced to a panel of judges who, like the authors, are deeply passionate about writing. We are profoundly grateful for the judges: Joel Armstrong, Terri DeBoer, Caitlin Horrocks, Trinity McFadden, Jodi McKay, Mike Salisbury, Janyre Tromp and Jay Whistler.

We are also deeply grateful to Gary D. Schmidt for providing the foreword to this anthology and delivering the keynote address at the 2024 Write Michigan Short Story Awards Ceremony.

The generous support and partnership of Schuler Books, Canton Public Library, Capital Area District Library and the Michigan Learning Channel has been exceptionally valuable to KDL in reaching out and inviting authors from across the state to participate in this year's contest.

Thanks also to the Write Michigan Committee for tirelessly organizing, promoting and bringing fun to the short story contest: Brad Baker, Amber Elder, Keeva Filipek, Randy Goble, Janice Greer, Josh Mosey, Lauren Hagerman Tekelly, Deb Schultz, Remington Steed and Katie Zuidema.

Lance Werner, Executive Director of Kent District Library, and Bill and Cecile Fehsenfeld, owners of Schuler Books, have been steadfast champions of this project since day one.

Our appreciation goes to artist Adolfo Valle for providing us with the beautiful Write Michigan artwork. See more of his work at **adolfovallestudios.com**.

Ultimately, thanks go to you, our readers, for reading and voting on finalists, telling others about the contest, visiting libraries around the state and encouraging writers to put their words on paper to share the power of expression through short stories.

Amber Elder, Kent District Library
Pierre Camy, Schuler Books

Sponsors

SCHULER BOOKS

Chapbook Press

Kent District Library

Canton Public Library

Schuler Books
Self-Publishing Services

Thanks to Schuler Books' Espresso Book Machine, we can help you print your book. You provide us with two PDF files (one for the cover and one for the text or bookblock) and we will print a high-quality paperback book for you, in color or black and white. The Espresso Book Machine can print books from 40 pages to 650 pages long.

What are the benefits of printing your work with Schuler Books?

- This is your book.
- You'll receive one-on-one support
- Since you sign a non-exclusive contract with us, you may pursue any other publishing venture that you choose.
- You retain all rights to the printed work, and you have complete control over layout, content and design.
- No minimums. You may print one copy or as many as you want.
- You retain rights for non-exclusive distribution and may sell books printed at Schuler Books or with the Chapbook Press through any avenue.
- Modifications are allowed at any time, for an additional fee.
- You set the book price and determine the royalty per book.

What we need to print your book

2 print-ready PDF files: one for the book and one for the cover, formatted the way you want them to look. We will upload your files and print a paperback edition of your book on high quality (archival) paper and a full-color glossy cover, in any size you want from 5"x 5" to around 8" x 10.5"

We can help you get there

We can help as much or as little as needed in each area of making your book a reality.

New Services:

- e-Book /Global distribution print and digital package: Your title (in print or as an eBook) will be available for purchase to over 39,000 global retailers, and their customers. The eBook will be available for more than 70 different
Ereaders including Amazon Kindle, Apple iBookstore, Barnes&Noble NOOK, Kobo, Sony, etc.) Bookstores and retailers around the world will be able
to order your book for their customers.
- Title set-up:
  - Book and e-book: $520 (includes 2 ISBNs)
  - Book only: $420 (include 1 ISBN)
You need to order a minimum of 50 copies within 60 days of title set-up.
Additional orders (minimum quantity of 10), require a three week notice.
- Epub Conversion: $0.80 per page (page count is based on the total number of pages in your bookblock)
  - Conversion will take three weeks.
  - For Printing costs and author compensation please ask for a quote.

Chapbook Press

Chapbook Press

	Short Run	Standard Package	Chapbook Press Publishing
	$50 Plus Production Costs	**$150** Plus Production Costs	**$300** Plus Production Costs
Maximum Print Run	20 Copies	Unlimited	Unlimited
Page Maximum	100 Pages	650 Pages	650 Pages
Personal Consultation	30 Minutes	30 Minutes	60 Minutes
Email Support	Limited Support	Included	Included
PDF Review	No	No	Yes
Proof Copy	1 Proof Copy	1 Proof Copy	1 Proof Copy
PDF Upload	Includes initial upload No Re-uploads	Includes initial upload +1 Re-upload	Includes initial upload +1 Re-upload
Cover	Basic Text Cover	Basic Template Cover	Basic Template Cover
Saved for Re-prints	No	Yes	Yes
ISBN/Barcode	No	No	Yes
Library of Congress Reg.	No	No	Yes
Books in Print Reg.	No	No	Yes
Sale: Schuler Books	No	No	Yes
Sale: SchulerBooks.com	No	No	Yes
Production Costs	$7.00 per copy flat rate	$6.00 per copy +$0.03 per page	$6.00 per copy +$0.03 per page
Color Interior	No	+$0.15 per page	+$0.15 per page

A la Carte Sevices

PDF alterations (re-uploads): $25 (+ price of proof copy)
Scanning: $50 deposit / $50 per hour
File conversion to PDF: $5
Cover from template: $50 (prepay)
ISBN & barcode acquisition: $100
Amazon listing: $50
Library of Congress Registration: $50
Additional consultation time: $40 per hour
Additional PDF adjustments: $60 per hour

Freelance Fees

Pre-press file consulting: $15 per 1/4 hour
Manuscript evaluation: $250
Manuscript editing: $135 deposit, $45 per hour
Proofreading: $105 deposit, $35 per hour
Transcribing: $105 deposit, $35 per hour
Coaching: $50 deposit, $50 per hour
Custom cover design: $100 deposit, $50 per hour
Page layout: $100 deposit, $50 per hour
Hardcover Binding: Ask for a quote.

For more information visit SchulerBooks.com
Want to talk to someone? Call us today at 616-942-7330 x558,
or email us at: printondemand@schulerbooks.com

www.ingramcontent.com/pod-product-compliance
Lightning Source LLC
Chambersburg PA
CBHW071943190726
48293CB00004B/1318